In her long and prolifi[c] ... had intimate experience of the theater and book and magazine publishing. She was the author of two Broadway plays and a partner in a producing company. Now, in this posthumously published novel, she takes her readers into that fascinating world, a world as shifting and glimmering as a rainbow. Her storytelling magic illuminates the tale like a spotlight, and displays her in a genre new to most of her readers.

THE RAINBOW
was originally published by The John Day Company, Inc.

Pearl S. Buck

The Rainbow

PUBLISHED BY POCKET BOOKS NEW YORK

THE RAINBOW

John Day edition published 1974

POCKET BOOK edition published March, 1976

Ł

This POCKET BOOK edition includes every word contained
in the original, higher-priced edition. It is printed from
brand-new plates made from completely reset, clear, easy-to-
read type. POCKET BOOK editions are published by POCKET
BOOKS, a division of Simon & Schuster, Inc., 630 Fifth
Avenue, New York, N.Y. 10020. Trademarks registered
in the United States and other countries.

The precise position of a rainbow depends upon the location of the observer. Though fifty people see a rainbow at the same time, each is looking at his own particular rainbow, visible only to him.

The Ocean of Air
by David I. Blumenstock

"Goodnight, Mr. Potter, and happy birthday."

"Goodnight, Mr. Potter, and many happy returns."

"Goodnight, sir—goodnight, Mr. Potter."

"Goodnight," Henry Potter said. "Thank you all. It was a very pleasant way to celebrate not only my fiftieth birthday, but the opening of our new building."

A murmur of voices, the smiling faces of the scores of people dependent upon him, and he stood waiting, outwardly calm and confident, inwardly—oh God, inwardly how sick of them and sick of everything, even this huge new building, this immense new monument of glass and steel, towering above other monuments of glass and steel, all new here on old Park Avenue, New York! But he had learned long ago to put on the armor of his defense. He was an actor, playing his part in the world about him—what was that old thing Shakespeare had said about all the world being a stage? He had not read Shakespeare since college.

They were gone at last, all except Marie O'Brien, his secretary. She lingered as she always did, asserting her right over him, her possession of him. Plain-faced, sharp-tongued, two years older than he was, he knew very well that she had made him her life and this without the slightest return on his part, except the check she received every week and a bonus at Christmastime. She might have married, he supposed, although it was possible that no one had ever asked her to marry him. Plenty of plain women married, nevertheless, but he knew that she had no room for any other man, a sacrifice, he supposed reluctantly, but he had not asked it of her, and had not wanted it. He had never allowed personal relationships with his employees.

"Anything else, Mr. Potter?"

He turned away from her. "Nothing, thanks, Marie. I'll bet you engineered this whole party."

Her voice in reply was more than usually hard and dry, which meant that she was fighting sentimental tears. "It's no more than you deserve, Mr. Potter—after all these years! The best boss—"

He could bear no more. "Thanks—and goodnight, Marie."

"Goodnight, Mr. Potter."

The door closed behind her and he sat down in the big chair, leather and chromium, behind the desk as big as a tennis court, he thought contemptuously. At any rate he was out of the dark old building on lower Fifth Avenue where his father and grandfather had carried on the business. He had made his own house, and now that it was done, he felt lost and empty. Fifty years old and there was nothing more to do! Everything he had planned was finished. The soap and detergent company he had inherited he had expanded into a great industry of cleaning machines, designed not only for housewives in ranch houses and split levels, but for enormous skyscrapers in the great cities between the two oceans. Potter subsidiaries rolled the tide of profits into these, his central offices. He had no idea of how much he was worth in solid cash and cared nothing because he wanted nothing. No, he had not had time to think of what he might want if he had to think!

Well, now he had time. He had done all he planned. So what did he not have?

Children? No, he had no children. Once, years ago, his childlessness had caused him a haunting pain, but now no more. There was no one to blame. Ethel, his wife, had simply not conceived, for reasons that doctors had not been able to discover. He had, when he was thirty-five, submitted to the indignity of having his own semen examined and had taken comfort in the knowledge that he was not at fault. He was healthy and sound to the last cell of his being. Once or twice, too, he had talked with Ethel of adopting a child. They had been unable to decide on a boy or a girl and, undecided, the years drifted past them both. She was content now, he believed, a sensible woman, still good-looking, five years younger than he. She had a sense of humor and she never asked him where he had been when he came home late. Not that he ever went anywhere, or had anything to do with women, although years ago, for a few weeks, he had found himself involved, though mildly, with Adele Warbecker, the wife of his best friend. Ethel had smiled.

"Unless you're serious," she had said one night when they came home from a dance.

"Serious about what?" he had asked.

"Adele," she had said lightly, "Ed Warbecker's too good a friend to lose. Or is he?"

That was all, but the next time Adele had taken his hand he had patted hers and put it down. He was perfectly satisfied with Ethel and he did not want a strange woman in his bed. The seat of his discontent was deeper than sex. He wanted a change, a total change, and he wanted, first of all, a change in himself. He was tired of being Henry Potter. In a curious nondestructive way he was ready to kill Henry Potter and not by suicide.

He wanted merely to enter upon another stage of existence, to be, if possible, someone else. Last year, in a fit of restlessness beyond the ordinary, he had gone to India, ostensibly to show Ethel the Caves of Ajanta which he remembered seeing with his father after his graduation from Harvard. Illumined by memory, he found the cave paintings as enchanting as they had seemed in his youth. But Ethel had declared India insupportable because of the heat and he had left her in Darjeeling with friends, a retired English colonial officer and his wife, and then had himself traveled aimlessly about the hanging subcontinent, ending at last in a northern ashram in Almora, where without the slightest belief in anything he heard, he comprehended vaguely the philosophy of permanence within change, described by modern scientists, and the transmigration of soulstuff declared by the ashram saint whom he had chanced to meet in the railway station at Calcutta where he had sat fuming because he had missed a train.

The saint, observing him, had invited him, softvoiced, to join him in Almora, that peace might be restored to his soul, an invitation it would not have seemed rational to entertain except that the stationmaster announced to the saint that the helicopter had arrived, and the notion of accompanying a saint in a helicopter had been amusing. A disastrous few days it had been, nevertheless, and ever since he had been displeased with himself, even with this body, this massive frame, solid flesh upon big bones, this mind wearied with routine of machines and the management of men from all of which he was never free, however far he traveled. The notion, not forgotten since those few days in the remote calm of the ashram and the persuasion of the saint, that he, Henry Potter, might by some change become another creature, even upon another planet—

who knew, now that scientists had opened the gates to the universe?—was dangerously enticing. For years he had kept in the top drawer of his desk a small revolver as guard against intruders, and with reason, ever since one winter's night when he had worked late and alone in his office and a desperate young man, opening the door, had thrust a pistol in his face and demanded money. He had given the money, touching the burglar alarm set secretly under the desk, but the fellow had got away. He had not been frightened, only enraged that he could be at the mercy of anyone, and so he had bought the revolver.

Now he took it from its drawer and held it, regarding its smooth metallic grace, the compactness of its compass, as exquisite as a jewel set in steel, and meditated upon the spark of death it contained, a tiny force, a minute explosion, capable nevertheless of extinguishing Henry Potter. He toyed with the trigger, his finger tense, and was surprised to discover that he had actually to resist the impulse to pull it. A dangerous implement, this toy! He put it back, closed the drawer and turning the huge desk chair he faced the sheet of glass behind him, only to see his own image, mirrored against the lighted towers of New York. There was he, Henry Potter, the city his life and history—past, present, and future without end until his casement died and fell to dust, and tonight, at the end of fifty years, he could only go home to dinner with his wife, Ethel. They would dine together in the long dining room, alone at his request and waited upon by Beaman, their houseman-chauffeur. When the coffee was finished they would go to the theater, as usual upon any special occasion, driven there by Beaman. They would take their seats in the center of the fourth row, and the play would open before them, tonight a new effort by Carey Grange, a young man from Georgia, the present wonder, the latest genius, the whirlwind of Broadway. He had no faith in genius but the night must take its appointed way. He knew no alternatives. He sighed, wheeled his chair about, and rose and left the room without putting out the lights. He never put out the lights anywhere.

At nine thirty that evening Henry Potter squirmed in his seat. The theater was warm, but indignation warmed him beyond endurance. He looked at Ethel, sitting at his right. Her calm profile was unmoved, though how she could look at what was going on upon that stage, he did not know. Women were supposed to be so damned pure and moral, but here they sat, three-fourths of a crowded house, dressed up like queens and staring at a play about a criminal degenerate and a prostitute and lapping it up. Innocence or decadence? He puffed his cheeks in a sigh that was half grunt and leaned to whisper loudly into Ethel's jeweled ear.

"This is plain rot!"

"Hush," she whispered without turning her head.

He looked down at his wristwatch. Another hour to go, but everything had been done, the two had copulated, or if they hadn't they weren't able to, and it didn't concern him either way. Why did he have to look at a couple of bums he'd turn over to the police if he met them on the street, and certainly wouldn't let into his house? And he'd actually paid good money to come here and look at them! He fumbled under the seat for his hat.

"I'm leaving," he said in a whisper too loud.

"Henry, sit down," Ethel whispered back.

"I don't have to look at this rot," he said aloud.

A hiss of reproach rose like escaping steam from his vicinity. He paid no attention to it and clamping his hat on his head he stalked down the aisle. Let Ethel go home alone! Beaman would be waiting for her in the Cadillac. Bitter with outrage and fury, he strode out to the lobby and looked out into the street, where a few young men and half a hundred girls were waiting for the show to be over so that they could beg for autographs. Fools, he thought, fools, all of them, fools in the theater, too, to believe the fellow who wrote that trash, that rot, that unspeakable filth, didn't know what he was doing! The man was a prostitute himself, dragging his own foul insides out into the open and exhibiting them for sale. Here, look at my rotten entrails, that's what he was saying, smell how foul they are—only it wasn't entrails, it was something further down and twice as rotten.

It was at this moment that he perceived in the lobby a lean young man of dark countenance who stood with his hands in his pockets, gazing moodily at the posters attached to the wall. Henry Potter felt no interest in him and was about to pass by until it occurred to him that here was a fellow creature who had also been driven from the theater by repulsion. He paused.

"Drivel, isn't it?" he grunted. "Vicious drivel at that!"

The young man wheeled and Henry Potter found himself under the scrutiny of a pair of cold eyes, black beneath black brows.

"You don't like it?" The voice was unexpectedly soft, its fury obvious but subdued.

"I loathe it," Henry Potter said briskly, "and if you feel the same way, I'll stand you to a drink."

The young man gave an unexpectedly lighthearted laugh. "You don't recognize me?"

"I don't," Henry Potter said. "Should I?"

The young man pulled a program from his pocket and pointed to a name, his forefinger thin and long.

"Aubrey Dane," Henry Potter read aloud. "Never heard of him."

"That's me, I'm the director of the show."

"I don't know that I want to drink with you," Henry Potter said.

"I don't want to drink because I don't drink," Aubrey Dane said. "But I'll join you over a cup of hot coffee."

The young man fell in step and they walked out into the keen night air. Henry Potter drew a deep breath.

"God, it's good to get the stink out of my lungs! So you don't drink? How come you put on a show like that?"

"People love it," the young man said, "and I need money."

Henry Potter grunted. "You give people poison because they happen to like the taste of it?"

"I do," the young man said. "It pays."

"How do you know they like it?" Henry Potter retorted. "Perhaps they look at it because it's all there is. Have you ever tried them on anything else?"

"I wouldn't dare," Aubrey Dane said lightly. "I'm too young to go around crusading. And too smart, maybe! Why should I be crucified? No, No! Thank you just the same." He put up his collar and thrust his hands in his pockets and whistled softly.

"You ought to have on a coat," Henry Potter said. "You're thin as a rail, the wind blows right through you. Here—we'll stop at this hamburger joint. I don't eat hamburgers or anything ground up. And I don't drink coffee very often. Too much of it rots your guts. I'll have tea. I learned to like tea when I was in China on a trip."

They turned into a steaming small restaurant and

sat down. The young man seized a menu and was immediately absorbed. He looked up once to apologize.

"I haven't eaten anything all day. The star got temperamental this morning and I had a devil on my hands. That's the only thing makes me want to quit the theater sometimes—stars! Waiter! I'll take a club sandwich and a malted milk. And apple pie."

"Cup of tea and a chicken sandwich," Henry Potter said.

"Yes, sir," the waiter said, a greasy fellow or maybe it was only the steam. The place was saturated with steam, hot and wet.

Henry Potter forgot the waiter. "Can't you get another job?"

"I don't want another job," Aubrey Dane said. "The theater's my life."

"Why?"

"I don't know. It just is. Ever since I was eleven years old."

"Your people in the theater?"

"No . . . I don't know who they were. I grew up in an orphan asylum. Not bad, but an asylum. I used to make up plays about who I was. Fantasies. I've heard it said that everybody in the theater world has had an unhappy childhood and makes up fantasies. Can't get away from it."

Henry Potter considered this in silence. It had not occurred to him to question his own childhood. Happy or unhappy? What was the difference? He had been an only child, overwhelmed by love from his elders. They had made no demands upon him because whatever he did was perfect in their eyes, and he had felt no preference between his parents. His mother was soft, sweet, gentle—permissive they called it nowadays—and with her he had conducted small secret deceptions behind his father's broad back. Nevertheless both were relieved when the deceptions went too far and his father commanded them to cease. His father had been a real one, authoritative, but devoted to wife and son.

"People make a lot of excuses these days for doing what they want to do," he now said. "I don't see what a play like this one I just walked out of has to do with an unhappy childhood, especially in an orphanage."

Aubrey Dane sighed. His deepset eyes assumed an aggressive melancholy. "I don't like that play myself. What's more, I don't believe the playwright likes it. He just doesn't dare to quit writing it. It's pay dirt. Matter of fact, I have another play, entirely different, that I want to produce. I don't dare to. It isn't pay dirt." He brooded for a half-minute twirling a spoon in his fingers.

"What's it about?" Henry Potter asked.

"It's about a scientist and his wife. Nobody's killed, no adultery, nothing."

"Then what happens?"

"Nothing—nothing at all. The scientist's a decent fellow—makes you want to cry, he's so decent. You love everybody by the time the play's over."

Henry Potter was cautious. "I don't want to love everybody. Still, I don't want to hate them either."

The waiter brought their meal and Aubrey Dane began to eat in concentrated silence. The fellow probably gulped down all his meals like that! Henry Potter watched and sipped the hot tea, nibbling his own sandwich of dried-up chicken and even drier bread with the deliberateness with which he did everything.

"Where is this play?" he demanded.

Dane did not look up. He took a huge bite before he answered. "I have it in my desk."

"Where's your desk?"

"Couple of streets from here. In my house."

"I could pick it up," Henry Potter said.

He was amazed to hear his own words. What the devil did he want with a play? Nevertheless he had heard his own voice speak. He never took anything back—on principle.

The tense dark face opposite him suddenly brightened. "You mean—to back it?"

"Could be," Henry Potter said to his own further astonishment, and stirred his tea. "Depends."

"On what?"

"Whether I like it."

"My God—you could be interested?"

"Maybe—"

For the first time Dane smiled and suddenly his face was young, a boy's face. "Just sit here, Mr.—"

"Henry Potter."

"Mr. Potter, I'll run around the corner and be back in five minutes!"

"I'll wait."

He watched the thin fellow race through the door and into the night darkness. He waited, refusing a second cup of tea, and looked about him. Behind the wet counter two sleepy waiters sloshed dishes into a machine. He recognized it as a Potter product and looked away. In less than fifteen minutes the crowd would be coming out of the theater. He waited and Aubrey Dane was back, his face eager, a good face, Henry Potter observed, the mouth delicately cut, but the chin firm, the nose straight and fine. He came loping in, a manuscript under his arm, and dropped into the chair opposite, panting.

"Here it is! I ran all the way. When do you think you can read it?"

Potter had a queer feeling that he would regret all

17

this. It was not his pattern. There was a feverishness about the young man, wasn't there? He was letting himself in for something.

"Tomorrow?" Dane suggested.

"Tomorrow I have a meeting of my board of directors," Henry Potter said. He got up and put out his hand. "It will be a few days. Goodnight."

"I put my telephone number on the cover," Dane said.

"I'll get in touch," Potter said, and left without looking back.

Outside he paused to ponder for a moment. No, he would not go home to listen to Ethel chatter about the play or pretend to listen to him when he argued her down. That listening of hers, all pretense because she was too lazy to defend herself! Women were lazy. He felt a gloomy pleasure in returning to his habitual pessimism. And why in commonsense had he this play under his arm? He retreated into familiar melancholy. Tomorrow was less than ten minutes away, a day no different from the thousands he had already lived. There was no use in hurrying anywhere.

He paused in the moonlit night. The streets were all but empty, a few young couples sauntering, embraced. Ahead of him two old drunks walked, supporting each other, one on the edge of the sidewalk and the other in the shallow gutter of the street. While they walked they conversed.

"You awright down there, fella?"

"Awright, Pete—on'y I can't make out why I'm so short, all of a sudden—like."

"It was that las' drink done us in, buddy."

"Yeah—awways that las' drink done us in."

Henry Potter laughed grimly and silently. Young

fools, old fools! He passed the drunkards and remembered, as he might have remembered a young man dead too soon, himself the night he knew he was in love with Ethel, a night like this, clear and cold and a wind blowing in from the sea. He remembered the first kiss, the touch of her lips, sweet and fresh, a virgin in heart and mind and body. They had lingered at the gate of her parents' house, home from a motion picture—*It Happened One Night,* he remembered even that.

And why was he reviewing his life, an occupation one is supposed to pursue only when contemplating death? There was pitifully little to review, after fifty years. It could be done in a matter of minutes. He had kissed Ethel for the first time in the middle of his senior year in Andover. He'd gone to Harvard the next autumn because his father had wanted him to, and when he came home at the end of four years he and Ethel were married and he went into business with his father. In five years his father was dead of a massive stroke—the Fourth of July it was, and they had been standing side by side on Fifth Avenue, watching a parade. He was the president of the company after that and he could do whatever he liked. There was his life, all told, and what was the use of going on with a damned life like that? Ethel had said only yesterday if that was the way he felt about everything he had better see a doctor.

"What for?" he had growled. "Happiness pills?"

"Maybe," she said and had thrown him a shrewd glance.

No, he didn't want to go home. He would go back to his office and stretch himself out on the couch. Tomorrow, or someday, he would buy a ticket for—for some place or other, and take himself off alone to a part of the world he'd never heard of, leaving this play on his desk for Marie to return, unread. He'd find some empty island where he needn't look at fools, because he would be the only human being there. Then he needn't see again what he had seen tonight, the effect of the meaningless filth of life upon the crowd, their faces pale and empty in the reflected lights, pale and empty and silly. He loathed them all again at this moment. There was no health left. And maybe he'd never come back.

He let himself into the delivery door with his passkey. It had been a fad with him that he must have keys to the building so that at any time he could enter, if he wished, night or day. The basement corridor was dimly lit and he walked its length to the elevator and pushed the button for the twenty-fifth floor. So where was the night watchman? Asleep somewhere, probably, and tomorrow he would fire the fellow! Tomorrow? He would not be here. His nephew Bob would have to take over, as if he were dead. He could leave a note for Bob saying that the night man must be fired.

The elevator moved upward with silent speed, the machine efficient, but mindless. The thing would take a burglar as readily as the owner wherever he wanted to go. It stopped at the twenty-fifth floor and waited for him to leave. He stepped out, and the prompt door slid shut behind him. He walked along the deeply carpeted foyer and unlocked the door of his offices. The night lights were burning and he passed the desks of his staff to the two inner rooms, huge and handsome, where he lived most of his life. Someone had turned off the lights. "The watchman, doubtless," he muttered to himself. Perhaps he wouldn't fire him after all. He touched the silent button and the rooms flooded into the brightness of day. His cleaning staff had come and gone, leaving a faint pungent smell of detergent. His desk was in order and dustless, his chair waiting, the comfortable chair designed for his big-boned body. He dropped the manuscript on his desk, took off his hat and his topcoat, and put them in the closet. Then he sat down. He was wide awake and unutterably lonely and bored. There before him was the play. Upon the blue paper cover he saw a title, *Night in the Desert*. He turned a page. *Act I, Scene I*. Living room of a shack in a desert . . . He began to read, the first time he had ever read a modern play. It was easy, just people talking.

At three o'clock in the morning he finished. He put the pages together neatly and fitted them into the folder. Then he sat for long minutes thinking. He had not really thought deeply about anything since he had been in Almora. There was something here to think about, something in this play that reached down into his vitals and twisted them. It was painful but pleasurable. He wheeled around in the big chair and stared into the darkness of the city before dawn. The lights were out except for the glimmer of the streets and now he was not mirrored there. He was lost in the night. He turned again and dialed the telephone number typed below Aubrey Dane's name. The telephone rang for a long time. He was about to put down the receiver when he heard Dane's voice, very sleepy.

"Yes?"

"Aubrey Dane?"

"Speaking."

Henry Potter growled. "Sleeping, you'd better say! But you ought to be asleep this time of night so I won't complain . . . I've read that damned play."

The voice became alert and alive. "Mr. Henry Potter!"

"Speaking."

"You don't mean—you can't mean—have you actually stayed awake to read the play, sir?"

"I did and I don't pretend otherwise. I picked it up —and couldn't put it down."

"You can't imagine what this means to me, Mr. Potter. Shall I come right over?"

Henry Potter laughed. "No, I'm going home and get some real sleep for once. Be at my office at ten o'clock."

He hung up and sat back in his chair. He was an idiot, a sentimental idiot, but suddenly here was something he wanted to do. He wanted to take revenge on that staring, blank-faced audience there in the theater. He wanted to defy the criminal degenerate and the prostitute and sweep them off the stage. In their place he would put two people in love, sensible, healthy, intelligent people, trying to find a good life together in a threatened world. That was real love, the love he had once known with Ethel, and had forgotten and could perhaps renew again. If people could see love for what it was, they would never again tolerate the exposed entrails of a rotten and perverted human being. . . . And he wanted to know the writer of this play.

He tried to make no noise as he undressed in the bathroom but when he lit the night-light cautiously to see what time it was before going to his adjoining bedroom he saw Ethel looking at him with one eye open.

"Where have you been, you reprobate?" she murmured.

"I went back to the office."

She yawned. "No wife would believe that except me. But then no one is married to you except me. So I believe you."

She pulled the blanket across her shoulders and

slept again. He paused to look at that calm sleeping face. He remembered this woman a placid pretty girl, a haven of peace, comforting, consoling, sweet-tempered, and finally the most irritating human being he had ever known. He had loved her with fury and distraction and still did, but her calm never broke. There had been years when he had deliberately tried to break it and she had only laughed at him. Once when he had shouted at her that she did not know what love was, she had looked at him with perceptive eyes.

"Perhaps it's you who doesn't know what love is," she had retorted.

They had exchanged a long hard gaze and he had made no answer. They had approached crisis in this fashion more than once, her eyes daring him to meet her in battle, and he had always evaded the final combat. Women! They never knew when they had lost in an argument, anyway! In fact, it now occurred to him gloomily, she did not consider that she might lose, that she might be wrong, mistaken, unreasonable, absurd— all those probabilities which women considered impossibles!

He sighed, put out the light, and went to his bed. Of the two of them Ethel was certainly the more durable. He had been angry with her again and again until somewhere in their life together, about ten years ago, he had discovered that all his private passions and angers made no more change in her than if she were marble. She was not marble; she was soft and gentle and yielding, though fearless and unrelenting; she said merely that she only enjoyed being happy and making others happy. True, her definition of happiness was simple. To live pleasantly in a comfortable house and have no worry about anything, to make no superlative demands on life or on anyone, that was the sum of it for Ethel, a personification of commonsense, he thought gratefully when he was not angry with her. Or was she? After all these years he could not guess. And unable to know, or to guess, he found himself in love with her still, in a curious exasperating sort of way. At least he was in love with no one else. . . .

He blew a great sigh and was instantly asleep.

When he reached for the bedside clock, hours later, he was horrified. Half past nine! He saw that Ethel was up and gone. His room was in order. She had even laid out fresh clothes for him on a chair and he had slept through it all. He leaped out of bed and then sat down, aware of a sudden dizziness. "You take things too hard, Henry," his doctor had said. "You're in good shape, but you manufacture your own worries. You're not a boy any more. Stop leaping at life."

He closed his eyes and drew a deep breath. All right, slow down. Walk to the shower. Make the water tepid, not too cold, not too hot. Don't scrub your skin off with the towel. Shave slowly and don't hack at yourself. Hair getting thin at the temples and he needn't brush it as though he wanted to be rid of it. Clothes—his dark gray suit, white shirt, maroon tie.

Twenty minutes and he was alone in the dining room, the maid, Nora, serving his breakfast.

"Mrs. Potter said to tell you she was at the hairdresser's," Nora said, pouring his coffee.

He did not reply. Hairdresser! What would women do without hairdressers? He never knew what Ethel would come back with—an Italian look, a windblown toss, or what. These days her hair looked like a sofa cushion around her face. When he said so, she had laughed. "I think so, too," she had said, "but it won't last."

"Why do you have to look like every other woman?" he had inquired sourly.

She opened her blue eyes at him. "Why be odd?"

To this, as to most of her questions, he found no answer.

"I should think you'd like to look a little different from a million others," he said at last.

She had given him one of her long, smiling looks. "Why should I when I am one of them?"

He'd given up. He was always giving up with Ethel.

"Nora, my topcoat," he shouted now.

"Sure and I'm waiting with it," Nora shouted back from the hall. He took it from her, with his hat, and strode outside to his waiting car. The morning was glorious, a brilliant day, and Beaman waited by the open door.

"You took Mrs. Potter to the hairdresser?" he inquired.

"Yes, sir," the man replied. "I'm to go for her at twelve. She's having a permanent, sir."

Henry Potter did not reply. He settled himself and reflected upon his new venture. To one resolve he had made up his mind firmly. He would tell no one about it, not Ethel, especially, for what would she say to such madness? Nothing, probably, and he remembered her smile, her Goddess of Mercy smile, implying doubt and compassion.

When he entered the office Marie was waiting for him.

"There's a strange young man says he has an appointment, Mr. Potter."

"He's right," he replied, handing her his coat and hat. "He does."

"But I've—I've never seen him, Mr. Potter," she remonstrated.

"There's a lot in my life you've never seen, Marie, perhaps even Henry Potter," he said and brushed her aside, ignoring her stare of astonishment, even alarm.

A moment later behind his desk, he greeted Aubrey Dane, entering the door in a fever again, as he could see, burning with cheerful hope, as vulnerable as a baby.

"Good morning, Mr. Potter. What a fortress of a desk! I suppose that's what you mean it to be."

"I didn't make it," Henry Potter said shortly. "It's some decorator's idea of an executive desk."

"Some desk!" Aubrey Dane walked around it, admiring. "It's worth writing a play about in itself."

He sat down in the chair opposite. "Mr. Potter, I can't tell you what it means to me that you found something interesting in the play."

"I suppose you couldn't sleep the rest of the night," Henry Potter said, tilting back in his executive chair.

Aubrey Dane grinned. "I'm afraid nothing keeps me from eating or sleeping, sir."

Henry Potter stared at the young face, still vivid with hope. "You do look damn healthy."

"Oh, I am, sir. I hope you don't mind."

"Not at all. In fact, it's what made me read the play last night. I'd been to that sickly kind of thing you had a hand in and suddenly got fed up with everything. I was fed up before, but last night I was ready to vomit. So I read your play to see what you could do if you wanted to. It was like taking a dose of bicarbonate of soda on a sour stomach."

"Thank you, sir."

Henry Potter glanced at the expectant face and then looked up at the ceiling. Silence hung long and heavy between them. Evidently this young man did not intend to break it.

He brought his eyes down from the ceiling. "Well?"

Aubrey Dane bit his lip. The carefully casual exterior of his bright face broke above his inner intensity. "I hope you'll back the play, sir."

"Back a play? What's that?"

Aubrey Dane blushed a dark red with anxiety, which it was plain he could not restrain. His hands, clasped on his crossed knees, were white at the knuckles.

"Surely you know, sir."

Henry Potter stopped a yawn. "Putting up cash, I suppose," he said in a dry voice. He saw a pile of letters Marie had put on the desk for his signature and automatically he reached toward the handsome marble desk set Ethel had given him for his last birthday and began to write his name rapidly, on sheet after sheet. Same old letters! "Dear Sir: Concerning your inquiry of ..."

"I have never backed a play in my life," he said.

"But did anyone ever bring you a play before?" Aubrey Dane asked urgently.

"No, I have to admit that," Henry Potter said.

"There's always a first chance, sir. Maybe this is it. Something new for you, isn't it, sir? Different people?"

Henry Potter remained silent for a full minute, his stone gray eyes heavy-lidded under black brows, his pen suspended. He thrust it into its holder.

"Yes," he said, "something different at last. Damned if I won't try it."

The words spoke themselves and memory crept through his brain, to reveal the ghost of himself long ago. He was thirteen years old, a lean and awkward boy, tall for his age, his dark hair long, his brows even then too heavy and his mouth sullen. It was summer, a hot and monotonous vacation, in which he had noth-

27

ing to do, on his grandfather's estate on Long Island. The green lawns stretched empty around the monstrous old brown stone castle. Here he had been sent because, his mother said, he looked peaked and needed to get out of the city air. And one evening, idling along the street of the town, he had seen the advertisements of a theater where summer stock was playing. He had loitered, staring at photographs and posters. The play was a dramatization of *Oliver Twist,* and the announcement was of murder and mystery.

He had bought a ticket for fifty cents, and had sat through three hours of horror. Bill Sikes and his brutal dog, Nancy, the tender woman, slavishly loving, butchered, and left bleeding and dead—he had watched it, trembling and shivering, his heart as still as though it had ceased to be. *Were there people like that?* When it was over he had stumbled out and never gone into a theater again until he was grown and out of reach of his pious father.

He recalled himself now and wondered gloomily if that hatred and anger he had felt so long ago at the violence done upon the stage had lain hidden in him all these years. Life? Yes, it was life, or part of it, and the newspapers were full of such life, but his eyes slid over these columns. He was soft, maybe, too tender, except that he knew he was not. He could be as cold and hard as the next one when he wanted to—that fellow Al Payne, for example, whom he had deliberately ruined; Payne, who had been his father's office manager, and who, he found when he took over, was secretly building another company in the same business, using the name and connections of Potter Products. He'd found it out and then had let Payne have his head.

"Sure"—he had said, ferociously amiable—"sure, Al, go ahead, have your own business—why not?"

And Al, sweating and profusely grateful, had left him. And then with relentless care, he, Henry Potter, had sent his scouts, his private detectives, to ferret out every contract that Payne was bidding for and had sent in bids from Potter Products so far below that Al went bankrupt in less than two years, and had shot himself. This pursuit had cost Potter Products thousands of dollars but it was worth it, and he, Henry, had never regretted it. Al Payne had been disloyal and in big business that was worse than downright thievery. He came out of his reverie and slapped the desk.

"So," he said briskly. "What do we do first?"

Dane gave him his charming smile. "Money—that's always first, isn't it?"

"How much?" Henry Potter asked.

Dane coughed nicely behind his hand. "I think, sir, that for a play like this, just a simple straight play, you know, without much scenery or anything, and no more than ten people in the cast, it would be only about a hundred fifty thousand dollars, sir—maybe with an extra ten or twenty thousand just for good luck."

Henry Potter exploded. "One hundred and seventy thousand dollars for a play?"

"Things cost," Dane murmured. "The unions and so on—and actors, you know, especially the star, and I think we should have a real star for the girl's part."

"My God!" The words were a rising shout of protest.

Dane's face went white. "I know it's terrible, but that's the way it is," he said miserably.

"It's a crime," Henry Potter snorted. "For what I saw last night, to think that somebody put up a fortune, and people pay fortunes to sit in those jammed-up seats, where you're pushed on both sides—lord, a fat woman sat next to me and kept her leg-of-mutton on

29

the armrest all the time, so jammed-up that I could feel her fat heart beating against me. Wheezy, too. And for that I paid, mind you—and to look at what? Crime and incest and—"

"Yes, sir," Dane muttered. "Take it easy, please, sir. You aren't as young as you once were—"

"Keep a civil tongue in your head," Henry Potter growled. "I'm far from old."

The young man smiled, pleading. "You certainly don't look your age, sir. Maybe you'd better forget about the play."

Henry Potter laughed suddenly. "How old do you think I am?"

"I don't think you're sixty yet, sir," Dane said desperately.

"Sixty!" Henry Potter howled. "Why, I'm barely fifty!"

"Forgive me," Dane whispered. He looked over Henry Potter's head and through the huge plate glass window behind. Immediately his expression changed to one of dreamy pleasure. He forgot where he was. The office became a theater, Henry Potter a figure on a stage, an actor in a scene. He was back in his own world.

"Gorgeous backdrop," he mused aloud. "Towers reaching to a sky as blue as the sea. Matter of fact, it *is* a sea. The air, the atmosphere, is only a sort of sea and we are all in it. We're fish, swimming in our particular sea. The water fish, the silver-scaled beauties —they're ignorant of their own sea, doubtless, merely breathing it in and out of their gills in the same way that we breathe in and out—"

"So," Henry Potter said, subsiding as he breathed. "I have to provide one hundred and seventy thousand dollars?"

Dane brought his eyes back from the seas around. "Don't you have it, sir?"

"Certainly I have it," Henry Potter said indignantly. "But why should I spend it on a play?"

"Somebody has to, every time a play is produced on Broadway," Dane pleaded. His voice was a husky whisper. What if—but luck had to break for him somehow, sometime. He'd been too hopeful. He was always too hopeful. All theater people were, else how could they live the absurd lives they did live? He stole a look at Henry Potter. Henry Potter? He never dreamed he'd ever see the tycoon everyone talked about and no one knew, much less sit here in this monstrous office and talk about a play—not that anything really happened—probably wouldn't—a face as near rock as a human face could be—that jaw, those cold gray eyes under jutting black brows—

"Let's get down to business," Henry Potter said abruptly. "Who usually puts up the cash?"

"The producers, sir."

"Where do they get it?"

"Out of anybody they can—friends, maybe—"

Henry Potter looked mystified. "Friends? They wouldn't be friends afterwards. Not anybody I know."

Dane looked at him without reply.

"I won't get it out of any friends of mine," Henry Potter growled. "But I'll get it. I've done a lot of favors—until now. I'll organize my own play company and I'll get shareholders, that's what I'll do. I'll make a Potter subsidiary, only not for soap or dishwashers. And stop saying 'sir' to me."

"You're wonderful, Mr. Potter," Dane said. He was so shocked with surprise that he was bewildered. Things happened too fast with this man. What—all the money at once—the incredible sum, without picking up a few dollars here, a few more there, collecting promises, too, that might never be kept—

"Perhaps not wonderful," Henry Potter growled, "but I'm damned good at whatever I do, and don't you forget it." The old man slapped his big hairy hand on his absurd desk for emphasis. "I like to win, that's all! So let's have a winner!"

"Yes—a winner," Dane echoed in a daze.

"But look," Henry Potter said, "go home and read the play over. You could improve it. The girl could be a bit more—" He paused, frowning.

Dane waited. "Yes, sir?" he said at last.

"A bit more of a—well, a bit more adventurous— maybe, or—"

"Oh, no, sir!" Dane broke in. "You see, she *wasn't* —she *isn't*. It wouldn't be true to her—"

Henry Potter stared at him. "You mean—she's *real?*"

"Of course she's real!" Dane cried.

"You mean—you've taken some woman from life—"

"Oh, no, sir—she's real in the *play!*"

Henry Potter stared at the young man's face. It was anxious yet desperately determined. He broke into laughter, short yet grim. He could understand this young fellow not wanting interference with one of his products!

Ten days later the calm and traditional atmosphere of Potter Products was disturbed by small frantic men. Marie O'Brien, typing the usual letters dictated the day before by her employer, heard a hoarse cough at her elbow. She looked up and was alarmed by the face she saw, a rough face belonging to a rough-looking man who needed a shave.

"Say-ay," the man hissed. "Are you the boss's secretary?"

"I am," she replied. "What do you want?"

He pulled a soiled envelope from his pocket. "You type this?"

Marie took the letter from the envelope with thumb and forefinger. One glance answered his question.

"I did not type it," she said. "It isn't typed. It's been done on a mimeograph."

She read it. Could it be possible that her own employer, Henry Potter, had dictated such a letter? A play, and practically ordering this fellow, Jim Brady, to invest in the play! Fifty dollars? Potter Products had hundreds of truck drivers, and at fifty dollars apiece—

"Lady, I got a wife and six kids and I ain't got no fifty dollars to put in no play," Jim Brady pleaded.

"Of course not," she said. "Who has?"

"Lady, what can you do for me?"

"I'll see."

She rose, letter in hand, and went to the inner office. Henry Potter was on the telephone. She waited and heard him speaking a strange language.

"I don't know a goddamned thing about show business, McCann, but I've found a play that I want to see on Broadway. Yes, of course it's a big gamble. . . . Sure, I know it's crazy, I know that much. All right, send him in today, eleven o'clock."

He put down the receiver. "What are you goggling at me for, Marie?"

She held out the letter, speechless. Then it was true!

"Well?" Henry Potter said sharply.

She closed her jaws. "There's a man in the outside office, Mr. Potter."

He opened a drawer and took out a handkerchief and dusted a bit of cigar ash from his vest.

"What does he want?"

"He's Jim Brady."

"Don't know him."

"One of our truck drivers, sir. And he says you wrote him this letter telling him he has to put fifty dollars into a play."

"Well?" His piercing eyes burned into her small gray ones.

"I didn't write any such letter, sir."

"Of course not. It's not office business."

"You mean you—"

"I mean I'm setting up a separate office for the production of a play, a limited company that I can close when the play's produced—if I want to. It has nothing to do with you, except that I expect you to put your own fifty dollars into the play."

"But, Mr. Potter—"

He cut off her wail. "A share is two thousand dollars, so what's fifty? You'll get your investment back several times over in profits."

"Yes, sir, but it's scarcely fair—"

"I don't want to remind you that I've contributed generously to your family in time of need. Your mother's hospital bill—"

"Yes, sir. I'll be glad to help, sir. Anything that interests you interests me."

"Good! That's the spirit I expect from my employees. Have I ever asked you for anything before?"

"No, you haven't, Mr. Potter."

"Nor from anybody. But this is a venture—adventure, maybe. It takes the place of something else I was about to do—for the moment, anyway. I'll get some satisfaction out of it, as least. I have a grudge, I guess—the hours I've sat jammed into miserable seats, looking at trash, et cetera! Well, I'll have my own fling at a play."

"Mr. Potter," Marie said. "I don't know what you are talking about."

He dropped the ash from his cigar into a silver ashtray. It had once been a tray for calling cards, and it had belonged to his grandmother. "Quaint," Ethel said, "but useless now except for ashes. Why don't you put it on your desk? It would be rather romantic, wouldn't it?"

He had paid no attention to this, but later he saw it on his desk and here it had been ever since. He remembered his grandmother as a small, straight figure who ordered people about. Once she had ordered him to pick up his toys and he had refused to obey, although he had been only four.

"*You* do it," he had said.

She had slapped him, whereupon he had bitten her finger. When his mother cried out in consternation, the old lady had only laughed. "That's the Potter spunk," she had said.

He looked at Marie now from under his heavy brows. "Do you have to know what I'm talking about?"

"No, I suppose not. But I always have, until today."

Her lower lip quivered, and he saw it and steeled himself against a slight relenting at the edges of his heart. "Maybe I don't know, either," he admitted.

Marie stepped forward impulsively. "Mr. Potter, are you sure you feel all right?"

He laughed. "I never felt better. It's a great morning to be alive."

She stepped back. "You want me to tell Jim Brady then that you—"

"Of course I do," he said crossly. "Did you ever know me to change my mind on a business deal?"

She looked at him, considering an impossible reply.

35

Then she turned and went out, silent, and closed the door behind her softly.

Henry Potter waited until the door was shut before he took up the telephone.

"Yes, Mr. Potter," a girl said.

"Get me Bob Hunt, my nephew."

"He's in Jamaica, Mr. Potter. Remember?"

"I don't care where he is—get him."

He slammed the receiver down and wheeled around in his chair to survey again the bare brilliance of New York on a winter's day. Millions of people were concealed in that desert of brick and stone, those towers of Babel, people speaking many languages and communicating nothing to him. Surely what he wanted was simple enough. He was not motivated by hatred, not really. Hatred was no more than the reflex of yearning for friendliness and warmth and love from no one in particular, except someone human. It was very lonely here in the steel and glass castle, in New York, looking down upon people who were only ants at this distance. He wanted to touch life intimately, somewhere, anywhere. No one came into this office unless for business, or to beg for money. Letters addressed to Potter Products were for business or appeals for charities. As for the dinners that he and Ethel went to or gave, he was never lonelier than upon such occasions. It occurred to him now that he had always been lonely. The hurrah of college friendships had long ago evaporated. He thought about Ethel and wondered if she were lonely, too. He was sure she was not. Women didn't get lonely as men did. They took up painting or knitting or gardening, some sort of nonsense that filled their time. And they let their minds rest. God, how they rested their minds—

The telephone rang and he turned to it. Bob Hunt's voice was at his ear, surprisingly loud.

"Hi there, Uncle Henry—what's the crisis?"

"No crisis, Bob—but I want you to go into a new business with me."

"Don't flatter me, I couldn't possibly afford it!"

"I want you to take ten shares in a play I'm backing!"

"You—what?"

"You go to Jamaica, I back a play."

"Good Lord, I don't know anything about plays!"

"You don't have to know anything. All I want is your money."

"Don't force me to say it, Uncle Henry, but what do you know about plays?"

"So what if you lose ten or twenty thousand dollars?"

"Twenty thousand dollars? No, thank you!"

"A little more back talk from you, young man, and I'll double the price."

It was a joke, but he let an edge creep into his voice.

"Oh, all right, Uncle Henry." Bob's voice came with mournful surprise over the wires. "What's a few thousand dollars between us?"

"Nothing," Henry Potter said. "Nothing at all, so long as you cooperate."

"You are wonderful," Aubrey Dane said again.

Henry Potter was beginning to enjoy the sight of this brisk young man across the big desk. He came in once a day, usually early, before business accumulated, and the staff stared at him and accepted him, all except Marie O'Brien, but Henry Potter had settled Marie this morning, knowing her very well after all these years.

"Now, Marie," he had said, "don't you get any silly ideas in your head. I'm not losing my mind or falling in love with some actress or thinking of committing suicide. I've got interested in theater through my wife's dragging me to see plays that I detest. There must be some way of finding plays that don't stink like a rotten watermelon. Ever smell a rotten watermelon?"

"No, Mr. Potter," Marie said.

"Well, they swell up until they burst with their own foulness and then they stink. You wouldn't forget if you'd ever had the experience. We raised watermelons on a farm my great-grandfather bought in South Jersey. The soil was poor and sandy and it wouldn't grow anything except watermelons. It didn't even grow those until my grandfather imported Italian farmers to see what they could do with the sand. It was like the soil in Italy, as he noticed on one of his trips there. In two generations those Italians were growing so many watermelons in South Jersey that the whole city of New York with Newark thrown in couldn't absorb them."

He knew from her patient look that she suspected him of trying to divert her mind from some truth he wanted to conceal, and he chuckled. There was nothing he wanted to conceal from her because she knew him too well, or at least she thought she did, and the truth was he was tired of her face and yet was too kind, or too much of a sucker, to fire her.

He shuffled through the memoranda she had left behind her, contracts to be signed, orders for steel and chemicals, all the innumerable vast detail of a huge and successful company surrounded by subsidiaries. He shoved them into a drawer and the door opened upon Aubrey Dane.

"You're wonderful, Mr. Potter—so early in the morning!"

Henry Potter did not reply. He made an excuse to open an envelope lying on the desk—nothing important, a bill from Ethel's furrier for a silver mink jacket.

Eleven thousand dollars! She had said something about a silver mink, now that her hair was going gray. And yet in all the years of their married life she had never called him wonderful, nor for that matter had anyone else. He was not quite sure what to make of it. Dane said it as easily as he smiled.

"I don't feel wonderful," Henry Potter said at last. "I feel lost, kind of. You're my guide into a strange new world. You're a director, you said. Now what's that, exactly, in the theater?"

"Job definition?"

"Put it that way. Tell me first why you are a director?"

Dane bit his lip. "You've asked me something I ask myself every day. I don't know."

"You chose it?"

"I never thought of being anything else. I suppose that's a kind of choosing. I tried acting, I didn't like it. I wanted to direct myself. I kept seeing how the others should be directed. So I stopped acting. My first show was a flop. I kept right on. I've had three successful shows in a row. I can afford another flop."

"Meaning this play?"

"Yes. That doesn't mean I won't do my best to keep it from being a flop. But I wouldn't be honest if I didn't warn you to be ready to lose all the money."

"I've never lost money."

"Yes, well, it's still possible."

"Isn't it possible we might make money?"

"Barely possible in the theater. You can't count on it. You count on failure and go on anyway."

He liked this fellow, Henry Potter decided. He liked his cheerful pessimism. Under the intermittently optimistic exterior was a hard center of discouragement, perhaps cynicism, and, like a candle flickering above ashes, an incurable and youthful hope—or possibly, only stubborn daring, but maybe that was what hope was.

"Let's go," he said.

There was a long pause. He looked up to find Aubrey Dane staring at him.

"Go where, Mr. Potter?"

"Start—begin, wherever you go when you produce a play."

"Mr. Potter, I have to ask you an embarrassing question," Dane said in a solemn voice.

"Ask," Mr. Potter said.

"Do you have the money?"

"Yes, I do have the money."

The young man drew in a deep breath and expelled it in a whistle. He darted from his seat, seized Henry Potter's large hand, and squeezed it between both his own hands. "Mr. Potter, if you were a lady, I'd be compelled to—to kiss you!"

"I'm no lady, so restrain yourself."

They both laughed. Dane sat down again.

"I'll have to find an office," he said briskly. "I'll hire a secretary—get going on casting . . . get going on finding a theater—get going—"

Henry Potter broke in. "Why not operate from here? Lots of room!"

"Not wise, not play wise," Dane said. "Hordes of actors coming and going, waiting here for hours, all the riffraff—advertising agents, stage managers, everything—You don't know. It wouldn't do."

"I have plenty of riffraff, coming and going."

"No—no. We've got to be in the theater district, where we belong. It's another world, Mr. Potter—another world, and entirely different from your world. I hope you won't think it's a sort of underworld!"

Henry Potter had a sudden secret panic. Across his too vivid memory he saw a panorama of his board of directors, staid men, who probably never went into a theater except for some charity benefit cooked up by their wives. Well, it was none of their business, any more than he'd think it his business if one or twenty of them decided to sleep with a strip-tease girl.

"Suit yourself," he said to the young man to whom he was now committed. "You're the boss."

"Thank you, Mr. Potter," Aubrey Dane said. He rose with his peculiar elegant grace and Henry Potter observed it.

"You ever been a dancer?"

Aubrey Dane's mobile face expressed extreme repugnance.

"Me a dancer? Never! What do you take me for, Mr. Potter?"

"Don't get mad about it," Henry Potter said and grinned.

Afterwards, alone, he considered again his board of directors. They were men like himself, he supposed, and yet maybe they were not. Heads of big business, his competitors but also his associates, outwardly conformists, inwardly daredevils, each in his own way, innovators, capable of monstrous evil and great good! How did he know that Rosenberg, for example, that behemoth in the real estate business, would not enjoy an adventure into imagination? He grinned and pressed a button.

"Get me Moss Rosenberg."

He waited impatiently for the big slow voice.

"Good morning, Henry."

"How are you, Moss? Feeling strong today?"

"I always feel strong, Henry, especially when you want to talk to me."

"Fine, then you'll be ready to share an adventure with me—in the theater."

"What have you got to do with theater, Henry?"

"I'm sick of the shows Ethel takes me to see. I want to put on one of my own."

"Don't tell me you've written a play!"

"No—no, but I've found one. I like it. Want to put some money into it?"

"I never gamble."

Henry Potter digested this. It was his first impulse to deny that anything he backed could be a gamble, and second to tell Moss that he was lying. Only gamblers dealt in real estate. He rejected both impulses and made a different attack.

"You go to the theater, don't you?"

"Sure I go to the theater. Miriam and I love the theater, but I don't put money into it."

"You like the shows you see?"

"Not always. Mostly not."

"You're responsible for them, whether you like them or not."

"No, I'm not—"

"Yes, you are—by not putting money into better ones."

He hung up. Long ago he had learned that when he had made his strongest point he should hang up immediately. Let old Moss think that over! Meanwhile he decided that he would sell the formidable number of shares that he had in the Rosenberg firm. He'd sell them cheap, so cheap that people would be worried and follow his example. It was a habit with him to fight those who would not follow him. He buzzed Marie and waited for her familiar whine.

"Yes, Mr. Potter?"

"Get me my broker, Marie."

"Yes, Mr. Potter."

"You're damned odd, Henry," Ethel said to him that night at dinner. He looked up from his filet mignon. It occurred to him that most of their communication was over the dinner table but that was the way marriage went, and he enjoyed the way she looked at his dinner table. She was slender and handsome in her black lace gown. Her cool well-bred voice could use curse words and slang with playful disdain and sharp meaning.

"How am I odd?" he inquired.

"Cheerful," she said, examining him over a bowl of varied flowers. "I'm not used to it, I've grown accustomed to another sort of face—grouchy, you know. What are you up to? You may as well tell me before someone else does."

"I'll tell you in due time," he said. "It's business— a new outfit."

"Is that why you're never in your office?"

"You tell Marie to tend to her own job."

"She's worried about you."

"Tell her she'd better worry about herself."

"I'm not your cat's-paw, my dear love. Besides, I'm afraid of Marie. She'd kill anybody for your sweet sake, especially me."

He pretended to groan. "She'd kill me—for my own sake."

"You should always fire women who are in love with you, Henry. They're not safe."

"Does that include you?"

"If you like."

He wiped his mouth carefully with the large linen

napkin in his lap, rose, and went to her and kissed her. She submitted with grace.

"There," she said when he had seated himself again. "That's what I mean. You're certainly not yourself. It's not a bit like you, Henry, to leave your dinner to kiss me. Now I am really worried."

"Relax," he said.

"But I don't know what to expect!"

"Neither do I," he said gaily, "but it's nothing to worry about . . ."

He recalled the conversation a few days later as he inspected the new offices that Dane had found. They were in a dingy old building on Forty-fourth Street just off Broadway. The view from the window was of huge billboards announcing present, past, or future hits.

"Inspiration," Dane said, smiling. "When I get scared I look out the window. If they can do it, so can we."

He had established himself behind a small desk in the inner office. In the larger outer office a stenographer was already at work, a middle-aged pallid female creature whose hair was dyed a deadly black.

"You need it," Henry Potter said. "Where'd you dig up that specimen out there?"

"She's good," Dane said. "Knows everything and everybody here in the Broadway underworld. She worked with Grayson last season in his biggest hit. She's tough—she'll weed out the lost souls when we start casting—the drunks and dope addicts, the undependables, the impossibles."

"She could be any of those, herself."

"She could be, but she isn't," Dane said firmly.

Henry Potter sat down in a rickety second-hand chair. "And why are you in this pocket when the outside office is big and moderately well lighted?"

"Wait till we begin casting. You'll see rows and rows of people sitting out there. Lizard will keep them waiting."

"Her name can't be Lizard!" Henry Potter exclaimed.

"I don't know what her name is," Dane said carelessly. "She just looks like a lizard."

"You mean people actually call her—"

"Everybody calls her Lizard—Liz for short."

Henry Potter thought this over.

"What do I look like?" he inquired.

Dane shouted laughter. "Mr. Henry Potter! I couldn't imagine a more suitable name for you."

In such persiflage it appeared that business was to be conducted. There was nothing serious to be had from Aubrey Dane. He left after a few minutes, persuaded that Dane had been to a party the night before from which he had not recovered.

"I'll be here tomorrow morning at nine o'clock," he said.

"Heavens, no," Dane exclaimed. "The door will be locked."

"Where'll you be?"

"In my bed—asleep."

"What kind of business is this, may I ask?"

"Theater business. We begin at eleven o'clock."

"I'm always at my desk at nine o'clock."

"Good idea, Mr. Potter. A nice quiet hour."

"If you went to bed at a reasonable time—"

"There's no reasonable time for going to bed, Mr. Potter—only for getting up."

"What I see is that there's no use talking to you this morning."

"Thanks, Mr. Potter—"

He left the debonair young man and returned soberly to his own office and was filled with doubt. Dane was an airplant of a fellow, living on air, no roots, a showy sort, sparkling and talkative when he was in a cheerful mood and retreating into mysterious and shadowy silence when he was not. Was he married? Did he even want to be married? Had he any substance whatsoever beyond the strange willful energy that concerned itself only with the fantasy and make-believe of the theater? For the first time Henry Potter doubted his own wisdom. If the rest of the people in theater were like Aubrey Dane, would they not be as alien to him as though they came from another planet? If so, he would still be the loneliest of men. He wheeled his chair and stared through the great window. The day was glorious, and the sky as blue as a tropical sea, and against the blue the towers stood alive, alabaster and crystal and strong gray stone. Hell, he thought, I want to live . . .

2

That night when he was prowling about his house, Ethel asleep and the servants gone, it occurred to him that he had not read the play since the impassioned night when in anger he had left the theater. Under the increasing magnetism of Aubrey Dane's personality he began to be uneasy. He resisted the magnetism and wondered unhappily if perhaps his judgment were warped. Dane had praised the play and in the mood of praise he had read it all that night. Now, hardening himself against Dane's charm, he wanted to read it over again, coldly and slowly, without anger, detached as though he had no part in the ferment of production.

He was pleased to find occupation for himself, here at midnight, when he knew he should be asleep and freshening for a meeting with his executive staff the next morning. He decided, willfully, that if at his age he could not dispense with habit, he would never achieve a private freedom. He settled himself in his library, unlocked the cabinet where he kept personal papers and took from it the large manila envelope, sealed, in which he kept the play. Ethel was not inquisitive, but he had put the play away because he had no answer if she found it in one of her rummaging moods. Why on earth have you a play, of all things?—no, no, he couldn't face that. But the knowledge that she was in bed, her face a mask of cold cream, provided protection. He seated himself in the crimson leather chair by the fireplace, touched a match to the waiting logs, poured himself a drink from the hidden bar, and opened the bound manuscript of the play. He read slowly the cast of characters, a small one, the directions for the set, a simple set, opening upon a family scene: the scientist, his wife, and their child; the setting the New Mexico desert in the early 1950s where the scientist was at work in the atomic laboratory upon some project, important but unrevealed. He felt a faint distaste for the scientist. Such fellows were getting bumptious nowadays, lords of creation in a strange new sense of the phrase, fumbling around with their fingers in the pie of the universe—and looking the way Einstein had, an ancient beatnik with all that hair and an old gray sweater!

Then slowly it dawned on him that the play was not about the scientist at all. It was about the woman, his wife, a woman like Ethel who didn't give a damn for the man's work so long as she had her house nice. The woman was making curtains for the shack they had to live in while the scientist was working in the desert, and she didn't like the place. She was homesick for her house somewhere here in the East, but she was trying to be a good sport and make things livable, because she was in love with her husband and wanted to be with him on the job. She was a homebody, a housewife, a mother, all the right things for a woman to be. She wasn't an intellectual or anything like that. The only thing wrong with her was that she was a foreigner, a refugee from Europe. Her family had escaped during the war when she was a girl, and gone to England. There later she met a young fellow her own age, and he fell in love with her. But she was afraid to fall in love with a boy, and kept putting him off. Then one day he happened to be walking along the street with a professor of his and she met the older man, an American, a scientist lecturing at Cambridge, and she fell in love with him and he with her and they married and went back to America where it was safe and beautiful and she could forget everything that had gone before. And now, of a sudden, when she is making her curtains and fixing up her house, the husband comes in and says he's struck a snag in the project and has to send for the young fellow from England, who meanwhile has become a brilliant scientist on his own in the same field. So the young fellow comes over and soon he finds that something is wrong. He won't work, he won't help her husband, because he doesn't know what the project is for, the thing her husband is working on, and if he doesn't know who is to have control of it, the military or the government, or what, he won't work because he says he's responsible for the product of his own brain. And that sets her to thinking for the first time in her life. Her house, her child—what's the use of her spending her life on them if everything can be blown up in one instant? So there in the middle of the desert, in a most distant place, in the quiet emptiness far away from city or town, she wakes up to the universe and in it the world her husband has been creating while she's been making curtains and keeping a nice house for him. And when she wakes, she wakes up altogether and blames herself and the two men. What explosion!

He read to the final curtain—an hour and a half. So that was the way it would be if Ethel ever woke up! He lit a cigar and smoked it thoughtfully. Queer how men and women met for physical cooperation and then parted! There was nothing exciting about his business, of course, but suppose he were a top scientist instead of a top businessman, would Ethel have been interested? What would it be like to feel responsible for continuing the universe? Could Ethel have loved him? Would she have shared with him such responsibility?

When he went upstairs he opened the door softly. She sat upright in bed, a lace cap over her hair.

"Ethel," he said gently. "I want to ask you something."

"And I say no," she said indignantly. "What are you doing this time of night not asleep? It's too late."

"You've guessed wrong this time," he said. "What I want to ask is if you would have been more interested if I'd been a scientist instead of a businessman?"

She stared at him. "Interested in what?"

"In life—everything."

"Are you out of your mind, Henry?"

He sat down on the edge of the bed. "I'm only serious."

She sat up, hunched her knees, and hugged them with her arms. "How do you mean interested?"

"In my work, or me!"

"Heavens no! What a silly question! A scientist? What would I do, married to him?"

She yawned, lay back on her pillows, turned on her right side, and pulled the blanket over her shoulder. It was the familiar gesture of dismissal and he went away. But not to sleep with his usual abandonment! Again and again he was wakened by that explosion in the desert, fired not by a scientist's torch but by a woman's fury. What she had created, home and child, the man could destroy. . . . Hours passed before he slept. For the first time in his life he was interested in women, not a woman, but a species. What would happen if they all waked at once?

He could not answer his own question, for what did he know about women, after all? Nothing, no one, except Ethel! He could not imagine Ethel waking up to anything more serious than her morning coffee! Other women—what other women? At least he had never known another and he had no intention of—but he liked, he really liked the woman in this play. Come to think of it, in some ways she *was* like Ethel, wanting the house nice, though it was only a shack in the desert. When the house was threatened she fought to save it. Ethel would do that—only the house was not threatened, of course. After all, he mustn't take this damn play so seriously. It wasn't real life—or was it? Maybe it was—

"I could never run my business the way you run yours," Henry Potter grumbled.

Aubrey Dane smiled and at the same time lifted the receiver from a second telephone. He went on with a conversation across the continent, to Hollywood.

"I'm delighted that Nathan Couley likes the play. He's our first choice, of course. The part could have been written for him. At the same time, if he's tied up there until May—well, it's simply too late. We're determined to get the play on Broadway before the season closes . . . Yes, we do have the money! Yes, all of it!"

He hung up. "They can't believe we have the money. It always seems impossible."

He attached the other receiver to his ear. "Hello, Steiner! No, I don't want him. I want a stage manager who's had lots of experience. This is an out-of-the-ordinary play and I can't look after a stage manager. He must look after me. . . . No—no, I don't want Bill. See if you can get Chess Bates. I don't care if he's in another show."

He hung up. "It's a matter of coordination, Mr. Potter. Once you have the money—and the play, of course—you have almost everything, but not quite. You need a theater and a few actors. A theater comes first. Actors are hanging on every limb but not theaters. Oh no! Shows can close out of town—after fine notices and everything—because in the whole city of New York there isn't a theater to be had. Just let a breath of gossip get around that a play is not what's called 'commercial' and theaters sink underground. We don't have a theater, Mr. Potter."

"Who's the man to see?"

Dane scrawled a name and address on a scrap of paper. "Use all your influence, Mr. Potter—use your father and your grandfather and your clients."

"You'll have to be satisfied with me."

"I'm just warning you," Aubrey Dane said. "It'll be tough, but maybe you, with your name, can pull it off. His secretary wouldn't let me in the door."

Equipped with the scrap of paper, Henry Potter found himself a quarter of an hour later on the third floor of another building off Broadway, in a shabby, comfortable lobby, where behind a small desk sat an aging woman with dyed yellow hair. She was looking at a magazine and gave him only a glance.

"Come in," she said. "He'll see you in a couple of minutes."

Henry Potter sat down carefully on the edge of a rickety chair. In the inner office, from which he heard a loud bumbling voice, there sat one of the richest men in the country and one of the most powerful. Sidney Vallant owned eleven theaters and between his thumb and finger he held the bottle neck of the theater business on half the continent, Dane had told him.

"Nice fellow, too," Dane had added. "He collects Bach manuscripts. He's mad about Bach. But don't think he can be fooled or coaxed or any of that sort of thing. He's sharp."

"Any man that likes Bach is bound to be a good businessman," Henry Potter said. He himself liked Bach. You could always be sure there was a tune to a Bach piece.

Observing the shabby room now, the disorderly desk, the aging blonde, he perceived no trace of Bach. He sat in silence, ruminating, remembering the music room of his childhood home. At the grand piano, a gilt monstrosity first owned by his grandfather, he too had assiduously practiced Bach for his German music master. Music had been his mother's hiding place, her refuge, her spiritual food. She had been a small, precise, delicately beautiful creature, framed too finely for the world in which she lived. When people asked her what her husband did, she shrank from the grubby truth. "He's in business," she always said distantly.

The door to the inner office opened. An immensely fat man tumbled out upon feet too small for him, and crossed the room as though he danced on bubbles. The blonde smiled.

"Know him?"

Henry Potter shook his head.

"He thinks he's Jackie Gleason," she said. "But he ain't, not by a million dollars—plus!"

"Why does he want to be Jackie Gleason?" Henry Potter inquired.

She stared at him. "Money."

A quiet voice called from beyond. "Rose!"

She nodded in the direction of the inner office. "He's ready."

Henry Potter entered the inner office. A tall thin man sat behind a mahogany table at the end of a long narrow room, a beautiful room, he saw at once, but a withdrawn sort of room, the high windows curtained in wine red velvet, the floor carpeted in the same color.

"Come in, Mr. Potter," Sidney Vallant said. He had a pale face, lifeless except for black, heavy-lidded eyes. "I have just had a telephone call from Aubrey Dane— a promising young director—a bit offbeat, perhaps, but an artist."

"I'm glad to hear you say so," Henry Potter said. "I suppose he told you what I've come for—a theater, to make it short."

Sidney Vallant rose, shook hands formally, and sat down again. "This is a new venture for you, isn't it, Mr. Potter?"

"It is," Henry Potter said, "and I don't know why I'm in it, exactly. It's one of those things I do because I've never done it. I got sick of the plays my wife takes me to see."

"Which plays, Mr. Potter?"

"The last thing by Carey Grange, to be specific."

"Ah—yes—very good theater, though, Mr. Potter —very commercial—very successful."

"People have to see what is handed to them," Henry Potter said. "They have no choice. A few reviewers say what they like and the rest of us have to lump it."

Sidney Vallant looked pained. "I hope you aren't trying something that's not commercial, Mr. Potter. If you are, you're in for a very sad experience."

"Whatever it is, I'm in it," Henry Potter agreed.

There was a piano in the room, he now noticed, rosewood, with a pattern of inlaid ivory. "That's a fine instrument," he said.

"My father's," Sidney Vallant said. "He used to play it when he found life in this room insupportable. I do the same thing, myself. You care for Bach, Mr. Potter?"

"I ought to," Henry Potter said. "I spent hours trying to learn the mathematical fusions that he called music —great music, but cool and remote as the stars—as beautiful, too." He stopped, alarmed. Why did he reveal the lost side of him, lost in his boyhood, when he had refused to go on with music lessons because his German music master had told him his talent was small? He had forgotten that wounded young man, himself listening to the irritated musician, whose voice echoed out of the past now, "You don't put the piece together, Henry!"

Sidney Vallant's handsome mouth opened in astonishment. He rose, leaned on his hands on the table, and looked grave. "Mr. Potter, what is a man like you doing in the cleaning machinery business?"

"I might put the same question to you about theaters," Henry Potter said. "I was born to it—ancestral."

"Ah, true—this is the only business I know," Vallant replied. "My grandfather and my father and then I—"

"Same thing in my family," Henry Potter said. "My grandfather and my father and I, but I put machinery in place of theaters. Much as I hate plays, I've yielded to some sort of magic instead of doing a number of other things I could have done. I have twenty subsidiary companies."

The two men exchanged shy looks. "Do you know this particular bit of Bach?" Sidney Vallant asked after a moment. "It's a fugue that's just been discovered. I bought it in a remote little town in Germany—it was in the museum there but they wanted to build a new wing, and had no money—so I had the money."

"Same thing with me now and this play," Henry Potter said.

Vallant seemed not to hear. He drew a sheet of brown paper from the drawer in the table and went to the piano and began to play with a strong and gentle touch, a musician, and Henry Potter recognized him at once. He knew music when he heard it and he listened, transported into that far and tragic world of the spirit denied. Not that it was Bach's world, he suspected, for what man could frame these clear and happy coordinations of sound, as perfectly balanced as equations in science, unless he were himself a happy man?

The firm and final chord sounded through the room. "How do you like it?" Vallant asked.

"It's Bach," Henry Potter said. "No doubt about it."

"I'm very glad to hear you say that," Vallant said. "It's the greatest praise."

"What about a theater?" Henry Potter asked.

Vallant smiled at him sidewise and sat down again. He touched a button and a potbellied old man ambled into the room. The light from the crystal chandelier glittered on his round bald head and cut shadows into the wrinkles of his cheeks.

"Hector," Vallant said, "what's the theater situation?"

"Bad, Mr. Sidney," the old man said cheerfully. He walked to the table and unrolled a large sheet of drawing paper. "Every one of 'em is busy."

Sidney Vallant studied the sheet, took up a pencil, and marked five heavy crosses on various spots.

"Three out of these five will close."

"Yep," the old man said in the same cheerful voice. "Maybe the whole five of 'em."

"I prefer to deal in certainties," Vallant said. "Three. Well, the first theater to close is to go to Mr. Henry Potter." He rose and put out his hand. "Good day, Mr.

Potter—and good luck. Have fun. It may be all you will have."

"That was all there was to it," Henry Potter said an hour later over the telephone to Aubrey Dane.

"It's enough. You're a magician," Dane said, laughing. "I'll just get a confirming letter and we're all set. While you were busy I was pretty smart myself. I stole the stage manager away from another show—Chess Bates, the best stage manager on Broadway. We begin casting tomorrow."

The door opened and Marie looked in. "Your wife's here, Mr. Potter. Want her to come in?"

Henry Potter hung up. "My God, why not, Marie? Did I ever keep her out?"

Marie put on a look of shrewd blandness. "How should I know, Mr. Potter? I thought you were having a private conference."

"Get out, Marie," he said.

And in a few seconds Ethel was there in her silver gray suit and the silver mink.

"You're a handsome woman," he said.

She sat down. "Why, Henry, what a thing to say to me!"

"Is it an insult?"

"Not exactly, but it doesn't sound natural. It's like being given a diamond necklace—you know something is wrong."

"Would you like a diamond necklace?"

"Of course not—unless you feel you must give me one."

Their eyes met in concealing banter. Why couldn't he simply tell her that he was backing a play? There was neither sin nor shame in it, yet he could not speak the handful of words and thereby reveal his secret excitement—not yet! On opening night, perhaps, though folly, for, of course, she would see his name in the press releases. He'd tell Dane that his name was not to be mentioned—

Ethel's cool voice broke across his dreaming. "What's on your mind, Henry?"

He woke. "Business," he said brusquely. "Always business—nothing but. How much money do you want?"

She crossed her slim legs. "I want you to come on a cruise with me."

"A cruise?"

"To South America."

"But I can't possibly. I have a big deal on."

"That's what I thought—some kind of a big deal. Are you telling anybody what it is?"

"No."

He caught her thoughtful dark eyes fixed upon his face and felt a blush rise from his collar. It was horrible that a man of his age could still blush, but he blushed easily.

She rose and smoothed her short skirt. Then tripping daintily on her high heels she came to his side and stooped to kiss his cheek.

"Have fun," she said. "And come back to me if you want to."

She turned but he caught her around the waist in encircling arms. "You aren't hurt?"

She laughed and removed his arms gently. "Why should I be? You'll tell me everything, one of these days. Do you mind if I go on the cruise myself?"

He did mind. He knew it instantly, but he was too just to say so. "Oh no," he said. "Go on and have your fun, too."

They interchanged a look, a mingling of embarrassment, daring, and habitual love. Then at the door she turned back. She came to him and kissed him once more, but this time sweetly and full on the mouth. Before he could move or speak she was gone, closing the door silently behind her . . . When he came home that night the house was silent.

"Where is my wife?" he asked Beaman, who opened the door as usual.

"Madame left at two o'clock," the butler told him. "She left word for you in your room, sir, she said to tell you."

He went upstairs and opened the door of his room and smelled the sweet and musky scent of carnations, and saw a huge bouquet on the dressing table, red and white, long-stemmed, glowing under the full light of the lamp. They struck him like the sound of music. They were her message. He looked for a note, some written word, but there was none. Yes, there was—a card on which she had written, "Remember I love you."

One thirty sharp, Aubrey Dane had said, and at the Tenth Street Play House. He knew where it was, for he and Ethel had at one time in their lives made a business of coming to concerts here. That time, however, was before their opera era, and he had not been here in a long time. The old hall was to be torn down now and already there was an air about it of hopelessness and the end of life.

"We've passed it," he said to Beaman.

"It's right here, sir," the chauffeur told him.

Yes, there it was, a dingy entrance. He descended from his Cadillac and paused.

"Be here at five o'clock sharp, Beaman."

The man tipped his cap. "Yes, sir."

The huge car slid silently away and Henry Potter

entered the playhouse, a filthy place as he discerned within seconds and smelling of lavatories. To the left was a steep wide stairway, and in the dim light he saw that every step was filled with people, dingy people, he saw also in the seconds. He touched a young man on the shoulder with his cane.

"Allow me to pass, if you please," he said coldly.

The young man lifted an unshaven face in which his light blue eyes shone with a jeweled brilliance. He hesitated, then shrugged and moved a few inches. Step by step among the huddled people, young and old, men and women, Henry Potter made his way to the big swinging doors at the foot of the stairs. Inside he found darkness lit only by the stage at the far end of the empty theater. A few indistinct figures sat here and there in scattered seats. One of them rose and came to him. It was Aubrey Dane.

"Hello, Mr. Potter," he said in half whisper. "We're trying out for the female lead."

"You mean all those people on the steps?"

"No, no," Dane said. "They've just heard that we're casting and they're here on rumor and wild hope. The ones we're interested in are inside. . . . Sit down here. Tell me what you think. This is the tenth girl. The other nine were hopeless, but this one has something—I don't quite know—"

On the stage a young woman was reading to a dry middle-aged man, who, he supposed, was Chess Bates.

"Who is the girl?" Henry Potter asked. He hated whispering and in the emptiness his voice echoed.

"Hush," Dane said. "She'll hear you. She's very sensitive. These good actors hate to read."

"Why?" Henry Potter asked, no more softly.

"They don't like to think they're being put on the spot."

"They are, aren't they? How else can we know—"

"Hush!" He sat then in unwilling silence, listening to the girl. She was reading the big love scene, and suddenly it was ridiculous, all that passion thrown against the dry impassivity of Chess Bates. She was a thin frowsy girl, her narrow body encased in a tight short black dress which kept slipping off her shoulders. Again and again she pushed back her long hair, dark and unwashed.

"I can't imagine her taking the part," Henry Potter said. "She's ugly, for one thing."

Dane shifted in his seat irritably. "What does that matter? She's photogenic and makes up wonderfully. You ought to know—she's Elena Lonigan."

"No!"

"Yes!"

"But she's in the Carey Grange show."

"Yes—but not the star. She'll leave it if I say so. She'd be the star here—if I decide on her."

"You'd better make up your mind, hadn't you?" Henry Potter said sternly.

"You never make up your mind in the theater," Dane retorted. "Oh, if you do, you make it up again fresh the next day."

"It's a queer way to do business!"

"It's a queer business," Dane retorted. He clapped his knees suddenly with his hands. "God, how she can act! She's doing that scene superbly. Do you see it, Mr. Potter?"

"I don't," Henry Potter said. "It doesn't look like love to me."

Dane did not hear him. He shouted across the empty seats.

"Kiss him, darling—forget it's Chess Bates! I want to see how hot you can get!"

Darling? The word fell molten with meaning upon Henry Potter's ear. Was this another sign of theatrical corruption? Darling? A man called a woman darling only when there was something between them. Was Dane dragging into the play some illicit passion of his own? He glanced at Dane's fine profile. It was cold and set and told him nothing.

On the stage the frowsy girl threw herself into the man's arms and sobbed.

"Good!" Dane shouted. "Good—good—now one—two—three and *kiss*—and cling . . . All right! Thank you, sweetheart!"

"Good God," Henry Potter muttered.

Dane turned on him sharply. "What do you mean, 'Good God'?"

"She needs a bath, a shampoo."

"Who cares? She'll take one before the show."

"You mean you'll hire her?"

"You don't hire Elena Lonigan," Dane said coldly. "You implore her to take the part. . . . Not that I'll tell her that—or her agent, either. We're looking at fifty other girls, but I may as well tell you my mind is made up."

"What about mine?"

"Yours too, though you may not know it."

"I'm not used to having my mind made up for me," Henry Potter grumbled.

Dane relapsed into silence and after that they merely looked at girls. One by one they tripped on to the stage to read the same scene, facing the gray and imperturbable Chess Bates. The words of passionate love grew dull with repetition and Henry Potter wondered if they would ever come to life again. Yet they did come to life in one way or another, each time they were repeated by the girls, these girls, one by one, putting into the dead words some private warmth of their own, some small memory of their secret lives, or some dream not yet lived. He sank into a hypnotic watching, seeing them come on, hearing them speak, and going off again, like souls born to appear briefly and then to disappear. A strange world in which he had no habitation! His own solid existence seemed unreal as he sat here in the empty theater, the only sound the stealthy footsteps of someone entering and leaving, the creaking of the worn seats when someone sat down or rose again, and always the voices of the girls on the stage, one by one, striving to create illusion against the grimy backdrop hanging in paper strips of faded color.

Beside him Aubrey Dane huddled low in his seat, motionless, hearing and seeing only the girls, fashioning out of the raw unprepossessing human material some creation of his own imagination, the perfect actress for the perfect part.

"Thank you," he said again and again as the girls tripped off the stage. At the end of four hours he rose abruptly.

"It's Elena," he said. "The others are sticks." He strode away in a dream, forgetting to say goodnight.

Henry Potter sat, numb with time, reluctant to move and weary to the point of stupor. For a moment he wondered why he was here and could not stir. He should have gone with Ethel on the cruise and cured himself of this madness. He had a long moment of homesickness for her, for her health and cool sense, her cleanliness and fragrance. What was he doing here, alone in an evil-smelling old theater? He got to his feet and straightened himself to his full height and felt himself assailed by a fragile weight in the dark aisle. Someone fell at his feet. He stared down and saw the frowsy girl, looking up at him, her huge eyes reproachful.

"Aren't you ashamed to be so big?" she inquired indignantly. "You knocked me down."

"I'm sorry," Henry Potter said. He put out his hand to lift her, but she was scrambling up, hanging on to his knee.

"Look where you're going, can't you, lummox?" she said with real indignation.

She dusted off her brief black skirt. Her legs were bare and on her feet she wore a pair of old dancing slippers.

"You might look where you're going, yourself," he retorted. "After all, I'm big enough to see!"

She laughed and he looked down into a sweet ugly face.

"You have me there," she said frankly and walked ahead of him, her thin body swaying.

The stairs were clear when he went out and Beaman waited beside the car, a protesting figure in his uniform. There was a shrewd evil surmise in the houseman's cold gray eyes.

Probably the fellow had his guesses, which were entirely wrong, but never mind! He, Henry Potter, had no call to tell a servant anything. He stepped into the car.

"Home, Beaman," he said, and had no sooner seated himself than he saw the frowsy girl standing there on the sidewalk and staring at him. He rolled down the window.

"Can I take you anywhere?"

She shook her head and stood staring, her sea-green eyes wide under her tangled hair.

"It's getting chilly," he said.

She shook her head again, her frowsy head, its curls stirred by the wind from the river.

"That car couldn't get down my alley," she called.

They were all staring at him now, the motley crowd that seemed to be following her. Now he heard laughter, raucous laughter. They were laughing at him!

"Think twice before you turn him down, Elena!" a young man's laughing voice shouted.

Henry Potter touched a button and the window glass rolled up.

The house was strangely empty without Ethel. She was a quiet woman, stilled by some compromise with life, he supposed, the sort of compromise which years compel, but her presence was articulate and he felt her gone. He ate his dinner alone, served by the impeccable Beaman. They had always had a man to act as butler, and however the creature might change, it was nevertheless always the same slim middle-aged figure, gray-haired, gray-faced. Ethel disliked fat butlers, and there was besides the matter of uniforms. The man must fit the uniforms she provided, and she liked an English accent, though not Cockney. Beaman filled the bill.

He ate his dinner with small appetite and then in the library, over coffee, he found himself thinking not of the frowsy girl who had fallen at his feet, and had later refused his offer of help, but of Aubrey Dane. He lifted the receiver on the table at his elbow and called. The fellow would never be home at this early hour. He was surprised—the fellow was at home.

"Dane?"

"Yes, Henry—"

Henry Potter paused. It was the first time Dane had called him Henry and he was not sure he liked it. Nobody called him Henry except Ethel.

"Have you had your dinner?" he asked.

"Yes."

"How about joining me here for coffee and liqueur?"

"Where's here?"

"At my home—ten minutes by taxi. I'd send my car but my chauffeur is about to leave for the night."

"I wouldn't know how to ride with a chauffeur. All right—I'll be there."

He heard the click of a receiver and then rang for Beaman.

"I have a guest coming—Mr. Aubrey Dane. Bring more coffee, liqueurs, and so on—"

Did he imagine that the fellow gave a slight start?

"Yes, sir . . . Did you want me to stay?"

"I'll open the door myself," he said abruptly.

No listening ears upon his secret life!

"Thank you, sir."

Certainly Beaman was very swift, nevertheless. The cups, the Venetian liqueur glasses were there in minutes.

"Goodnight, sir," he said.

"Goodnight, Beaman," Henry Potter said.

Did he imagine that the fellow had a look of actual fear on his pallid face? He pushed the thought away. He was not used to noticing servants. They existed for their usefulness and Beaman was as excellent as a butler as he was a driver—so excellent that it was hard to believe he had not been a butler always. But this was his first job—Henry Potter remembered Ethel's telling of his confusion.

"I think it right, madam, to tell you this is my first job—as a butler, I mean," the man had said when he came to apply.

"I can't take the time to train you," Ethel had replied.

"No, madam," the man had said humbly, "I won't expect that. But I've observed, madam, and I think—"

"If you think, you'll be an unusual butler," Ethel had said with a short laugh.

There was something she had liked about the man—clean-shaven, middle height, inconspicuous—a born butler, one would say.

"Very well—we'll give you a try."

"Thank you, madam," Beaman had replied.

That had all taken place eight years ago, and the man had become a fixture in the house.

Waiting for the doorbell to ring, it occurred to Henry now that he was bringing his secret life into this house, in the form of Aubrey Dane, a performance impossible if Ethel had been at home.

Someday, of course, she would find out, or, more likely, he would feel compelled to tell her. There was something about her placid clarity that induced him to total honesty with her, an uncomfortable honesty for he did like to feel compelled, and perversely, for she did not, in fact, make the slightest demand on him. She was herself so honest, perhaps, that she made anything else impossible.

The doorbell rang at this instant and he went into the hall and opened it. There Aubrey Dane stood, slender as an arrow and as direct.

"Come in," Henry Potter said.

They walked into the library and he motioned Dane to a chair.

"My wife's away. I'd like just to talk."

"Of course," Dane said.

He sat upright in a gold brocaded armchair, slim and graceful, his dark eyes watchful, and Henry Potter did not know how to begin. If Ethel were here, she would be setting him at ease, asking just the right questions. He imagined her now, lying somewhere in the sun on the deck of a cruise ship, thinking of heaven knows what. It had been a long time since he had inquired into Ethel's thoughts, and he almost wished again that he had told her before she went off what he was doing. And yet, suppose that by the time she came back he was a success again, in his newest business, how she would laugh, and with what fondness! He felt suddenly homesick for her. In a vague way she was his home and this house was nothing without her. He glanced at Dane and as though in answer Dane spoke.

"What's the function of the theater, Mr. Potter?"

Dane's eyes were thoughtful and Henry Potter considered.

"To make people happy?" he inquired.

"Define 'happy,' " Dane said.

"The simplest definition is just feeling good, isn't it?"

"Feeling good about what?"

"Life."

Dane reflected. "Rather nice! Continue."

"Well, then—proud to be a human being instead of cynical and ashamed."

Dane shot him a shrewd and piercing look. "So what about the subconscious and all that?"

"Leave it alone," Henry Potter said firmly. "The less we think about it the better. The less we know about it the better. It's best handled by thinking about something else and doing something that uses all our energies in new ways!"

He got up and walked about the room and paused to look down at Dane.

"Did you write the play?"

Dane looked up at him. "No," he said, "I've been waiting for you to ask."

"Who did?"

"The playwright, whom you will meet one of these days."

"That's all you want to tell me?"

"It's all I'm allowed to tell, now."

Henry Potter sat down again. "Have your mystery, you mystery man! What I'm interested in is the play. I want a whopping success. At this time of my life, and by habit, I'm not inclined to failure."

"You'll know at midnight of the day we open," Dane said, "and let me warn you to get your fun as you go. Beyond midnight of that day there's no guarantee for success or happiness or anything else. There's only one question you need to ask yourself now. Should this play be produced?"

"Yes." His answer was instant and unequivocal.

"Very well, then! We'll continue with the casting at noon tomorrow."

Silence fell. Dane glanced at his host. What does a young man say to someone decades older than himself? Henry Potter sat stooped in his chair, suddenly old.

"Mr. Potter!"

He looked up. "Yes, Dane?"

"Why do you want to be in the theater?"

"Why do you ask?"

"I feel responsible—in case, for the first time in your life, you fail at something. The theater is like nothing else on earth—unpredictable! Three-fourths depends on the whims and prejudices of the critics and *they* are unpredictable. One never knows their prejudices! And I've taken the trouble to look you up in *Who's Who*, and I ask the question. I know who you are. I find myself liking you—respecting you."

"Good of you," Henry Potter said. He straightened himself in his chair and years dropped away from him. His voice was dry but inwardly he was warmed. Powerful and willful as he was, it was seldom that he heard a word of personal praise. Odd, when he thought of it now, but he supposed that people resented him somehow—too rich? Too much power? Jealousy? It was subtly wounding, nevertheless! He felt warmly toward Dane in spite of a mild scorn that he, Henry Potter, could feel flattered by a slim young man twenty-five years his junior. He poured a half glass of crème de menthe. "As to why I'm in the theater—if one can say I am—I suppose it's because a play can make me feel—anger, primarily, or at present—but something more. Alive, perhaps? But that's all right. The great danger is to stop feeling anything—in my circumstances. Suddenly I'm fifty years old."

Dane listened and he talked, led on, as he himself knew, by the fact that he had said he liked him. He found himself telling Dane of his business, the men who worked under him, the spontaneous growth of a huge successful firm. And Dane listened—intently, it seemed—replying now and then, until the clock struck midnight.

At the gentle music of the tall clock's chimes, a grandfather clock Ethel had bought in England somewhere, Dane rose.

"I've kept you up. But you've kept me," he said, smiling.

He rose and put out his hands and clasped the older man's extended right hand.

"We'll make a success of our play, Mr. Potter. I feel it already a success."

"Well, I hope so—why not?" Henry Potter said.

He followed Dane to the hall, to the door, nodded his farewell, closed and locked the heavy mahogany door, and returned to his chair in the library. There he sat for a long time alone. The fire was gray ash, hiding a few red coals, symbolic, he thought, of himself. Unless a wind from the outside blew upon the coals they too would fade into ash, and life would be ended. He had meant what he said to Aubrey Dane. He wanted to say the things he felt, or have them said, and perhaps a play could say them, before all feeling died. This play, not of his writing, did, in an odd sort of way, say much of what he felt. Science was all very well, and scientists were unexpendable, indeed, essential if people were to better themselves, and certainly the inquiring, searching mind must be allowed to reach to the uttermost limits of illimitable space. Hadn't saints and religious leaders been doing just that, throughout centuries, and with far less accuracy of data than the scientists? Yet somehow people had to be worthy of these noble findings. He believed they were potentially worthy, but they had to be told—they had to be told how good they were. Especially women had to be told, and that was what was true about the play. There a woman woke up to herself as a human being and began to change her world by her own change. Ethel, for example, so good to look at—yes, to live with—but was that enough, after all? Long self-repression and long forgetfulness of all except business, the mechanical complexity of his days had conspired to bring his life to quiescence all too soon. He did not know clearly what he wanted to say. But he knew very well that there was a force in him, a power of emotion which he could not himself release. He could no longer, for example, tell Ethel that he loved her, and he wanted to be able to tell her. It had never been easy and now it was impossible. He had sometimes wondered if he were able to love anyone anymore or even to feel compassion. He had become a highly efficient human machine.

He sighed restlessly and, pushing himself out of his

chair, he walked up and down the room. He wanted above all else to know if he were still alive.

"What are you looking for? You turn down everybody."

He was seated in the theater again the next afternoon with Aubrey Dane at his side. The theater was dark except for the stage but outside the day was bright with wintry sunshine, late winter but cold and with no promise yet of spring. Inside the theater the air was hot and dry with furnace heat.

"I'm looking for the indescribable," Aubrey Dane said abruptly.

He was staring at the stage, empty except for a few actors, now at ease, and waiting for his return.

"Don't be lazy. Describe it," Henry Potter commanded.

Dane stirred in his seat and did not reply.

"I want to learn," Henry Potter went on. "I'm here for an education. You're my guide and teacher. If I were taking you around one of my factories, I wouldn't leave you to wander alone. You wouldn't understand anything you saw, either. Man, you must give me my money's worth!"

"I'm looking for fire," Dane said. "Watch now—see this fellow coming on. Will he do for us? I'm thinking of our young scientist, the innovator, the born genius. Is he in this boy? I'm looking not for a flash but for the unquenchable sunshine of Parnassus. Will he light the stage because he lights the world wherever he walks?"

Dane was talking under his breath, his eyes upon the actor, who had just entered the stage. A handsome boy, Henry Potter saw—and something else. He was perhaps twenty, tall and blond and delicate in his movements, shy, withdrawn—but all actors were withdrawn, he was beginning to believe. They came out of a hidden limbo of their own. They were silent or else talked too volubly and always about themselves.

The actor began to read the part glibly but without color, as though he had read the words many times. Dane swore under his breath.

"What the hell—no, it can't be—"

"Can't be what?" Henry Potter inquired in a heavy whisper.

"I'm afraid it is," Dane said sadly. "Too bad, but I won't have a homosexual in a leading part. He can't play the lover."

"But surely—"

"Yes, surely! Too bad—he looks the part, too. But it's no good. You can't teach that breed! They're dead inside where the heart's concerned. No push—no heat —no fire. They can't create."

He rose and went to the stage. "Thank you, Melson."

The handsome boy stopped, dismayed. "I don't have a chance?"

"I'm sorry." Dane's voice was steel. "You don't fit the part."

The boy went white under the lights. "But my agent said—"

Dane broke ruthlessly across the protest. "I've seen you and heard you, Melson. That's all. Next!"

He took his seat again beside Henry Potter. The boy walked quickly across the stage to the exit, his steps precise and delicate.

Next was a handsome aging man, clean-shaven, dressed in a dapper dark suit. He announced himself clearly: "Jonathan Bent."

"Come in, Mr. Bent," Dane said.

The man opened a big briefcase. "I thought you might like to look at some of my photographs."

Dane interrupted him. "I've seen your photographs. I'd rather hear you read. Have you a script? Yes? Then any scene you like."

For two minutes Henry Potter listened to a pleasantly modulated voice. Then Dane broke in.

"Thanks. That'll do."

The man stood, graceful and hesitant. "You might like to look at some photographs of me with a moustache!"

"No, thanks," Dane said.

The man went out, head bowed.

"Tough," Henry Potter murmured.

"You have to be tough in this business," Dane retorted. "Tough when you know there's no hope! I can't make people into actors, not even when they have talent. I can only help them to help themselves."

The procession came and went throughout that day and the next and the next. On the evening of the fifteenth day, while Dane searched for his stage family, member by member, Henry Potter became aware of a numbing weariness. Since he had done nothing beyond watching the come and go of actors he could not understand this deep fatigue. The theater itself was depressing, emptied of the well-dressed crowds, the lights, the fanfare of performers with an audience. Here he sat in the vast dim space, alone except when Dane remembered him and came to make talk across the uninhabited rows of seats, and even this desultory companionship grew less as the director narrowed his choices.

On this evening, when for an-hour he had sat in silence, Henry Potter decided suddenly that he could not look at one more actor. He was emotionally exhausted. Ruthless as he had been in his own business, he had never come face to face with those whom he rejected or destroyed. Even Al Payne he had never met after he had walked out of the office. He had not seen the sick look, the panic, the despair, the heartbreaking pretense of gaiety when a shrinking, frightened creature puts forth its best, facing what deprivation, what poverty, could only be imagined. Had he himself, for example, to walk upon that huge bare platform under the cruel glare of the uncurtained light, had he to read from a manuscript held in trembling hands, drive himself to pretend that he was a lover, a scientist, a bold young man, he would quietly have killed himself first. He began to hate Aubrey Dane. He felt a passionate pity for the men and women whom he dismissed. That cold and repetitious "Thank you," so utterly devoid of feeling, the sharp final appraisal, out of the many only the few told to wait, or even to come again—no, he could endure no more. When Dane had fixed upon the ones he wanted, then for him the play would begin.

He rose and went quietly out of the theater. Dane did not notice his departure. No one saw him until stumbling up the stairway, his foot struck something soft, and he heard a small cry of pain. He looked down and saw a huddled figure of a girl.

"I'm sorry," he said. "Did I hurt you?"

"Only my shin."

He looked down into a pale oval face, and recognized Elena Lonigan.

"Why are you sitting here alone?" he demanded.

"I'm waiting for Aubrey to tell me I can have the part."

"Hasn't he told you yet?"

"No."

"How long have you been waiting?"

"I don't know. Hours maybe."

"But surely you don't have to?"

"No, and my agent would kill me if he knew. But I've got to have the part. I never wanted a part so much before. And he's just doing this on purpose."

"He?"

"Aubrey. He has a mean streak in him."

Henry Potter hesitated. "Do you mind if I sit down beside you?"

"No." She drew her full skirt aside.

He sat down carefully. "How is he mean?"

"Directors are mean, I suppose. They have to be, in a way. Otherwise they couldn't keep the upper hand. And somebody has to be in control—I know that. But it's more than that with Aubrey."

"You know him well?"

"He has a reputation."

"For meanness?"

"For being successful. You take it all together. If he weren't mean, he couldn't be so successful."

He saw her pensive profile, perfectly outlined against the black wall of the stairwell.

"Just what is this meanness?"

She paused, twisting and untwisting her small thin hands. "I don't know how to say things. But why is he letting me sit here and wait?"

"Does he know you're here?"

"Oh, he knows! There's nothing he doesn't see and know. Goddamn, I've tried not to let him see how much I want this part, but he sees through me in a minute and he knows I know it. So he's letting me wait."

"Why?"

"He'll say it's because he'll make my agent take less money for me. But the real reason is because he wants to be in control of me from now until opening night."

"Control of you?"

"Complete control of me. He'll tell me what to eat,

when to go to bed, what to wear, how to walk, how to do my hair—everything."

"You'll let him?"

"I shan't be able to help myself."

Henry Potter was confounded. He did not know what to ask next—no, he knew but he did not want to ask.

"You're frozen, sitting here. Come and have a hot drink with me—soup, tea, coffee. There's a place next door."

She put up her hand and he drew her to her feet. It was a narrow boneless little hand, soft and helpless. She tucked it into his elbow and leaned against him like a child. He glanced down at her pale face and flying hair. She was very young and very small.

"You shouldn't be out alone at night like this," he said.

She looked up at him in naïve surprise. "Me? But I'm always out at night. That's when I work."

"Sleep all day, I suppose?"

"Yes."

They were out on the street. He glanced toward the big Cadillac standing at the curb. Beaman was asleep, his head tilted back and his face covered with a newspaper against the streetlights. He was glad of that—he could never explain. A few steps and he stopped.

"Here we are."

He held the door open for her, the wind blowing hard against him, and tossing her hair into a flying mass of dark gold.

"Oh, but it's good to be warm," she cried softly when they were inside. "I was colder than I knew, though I felt burning inside!" She turned to him sweetly. "While you're taking off your coat, I'll just go to the rest room. I've needed to go for the last hour, but I was afraid

Aubrey would come while I was gone. It would just be his luck—then he'd say I wasn't there."

"I'll wait for you," Henry Potter said and felt himself blush. What sort of sense did that remark make when a girl told you she had to go to the rest room? He hadn't heard anyone say that since he was a child. He gave his coat and hat to the check girl and sat down in a booth.

A waitress tossed a menu card before him. "Want to order?"

"I'm waiting for a lady," he said formally.

"Sure."

She drifted away. He waited, looking about the restaurant. If Ethel saw him here she would think the worst. Or perhaps she'd only laugh. He could imagine her, he could hear her cheerful, caustic voice. What on earth are *you* doing here—with the emphasis on the *you!*

Elena was back. She slid into the seat opposite him and smiled at him. The pallor was already gone from her face, or perhaps it was her freshly reddened mouth and the smoothed dark hair.

"What a relief!" she sighed. "I don't know anything more comfortable than going to the bathroom when you have to, very badly—do you?"

He received this inquiry with embarrassment.

"No," he said.

She was already studying the menu. "I'll have a thick steak, very rare, and a green salad. . . . No, I'm not looking at the Danish pastry—however much you beg me to have one!"

She looked at him imploringly over the menu.

He laughed. "Do have a Danish pastry! You're far too thin."

"You really think so?"

"I'm looking at you."

"Then I will."

He gave her order and for himself a cup of tea and she proceeded to further confidence.

"I eat a lot at night because I can't eat in the morning—shall I call you Henry?"

He swallowed bravely. "If you like. How did you know my name?"

"Oh, we all know you. Aubrey's told us you're our angel and—" She clapped her little right hand to her mouth.

He laughed. "And what?"

She dropped her hand and shrugged her shoulders. "Just to mind our manners. He says you aren't hard to it."

"Hard to what?" he asked.

"No, I guess, we're—"

She shrugged again and broke off.

"You're what?" he insisted.

"Theater people," she said.

"And are you different from the rest of us?"

He pressed her, curious to know her breed. She laughed, and shrugged again, thin shoulders half out of her low-cut blouse.

"We're—what are we? Bits of every part we've ever played. I see it in myself—all the girls—women—they all leave something in me."

"Memory, maybe," he suggested.

"Maybe."

The salad arrived and she lost interest in the conversation until her plate was empty. Then she took it up as she had begun it.

"I better call you Mr. Potter. Aubrey would think I'm being fresh—or something. Anyway, will you call me Elena?"

"If you like."

She laughed a pretty rill of mirth. "How funny you are! Do you know you look exactly the way a Henry should look?"

"Is that a compliment?"

"Yes! Henry sounds so reliable. Are you really very rich?"

He was instantly cautious. "Depends."

"You must be rich or you couldn't be backing a play with Aubrey. He has no money."

"So he told me."

"He was honest for once."

She drank a sip of water, put down the glass, and smiled at him again. "As I was saying, I never eat in the morning except for coffee. Then maybe I have a raw egg in the middle of the day, for my voice. I learned that from a little Chinese actress in a Rodgers and Hammerstein show I was in. She always ate a raw egg before she sang, beaten up with a few drops of lemon juice. I skip the lemon, but sometimes I put a bit of gin into the egg. Not always. I have a weak stomach. It's not weak all the time. The truth is I'm weak. I love candy. Chocolates. I daren't open a box for if I do, I finish it. Actually! Pounds! Then I'm fearfully sick, of course, and I can't eat for days."

"You need someone to look after you," Henry Potter said. "Where are your parents?"

"They don't approve of me, you know. I'm divorced. Twice. I suppose you know that. Everything I do is in the papers."

"I don't read those papers," Henry Potter said. Divorced! This child? "You look about sixteen."

She smiled at him, her black-fringed eyes enormous. "Thank you. I'm flattered. I was sixteen when I was married the first time. I'm twenty now—heavens! Old!"

"You're a baby," he muttered.

She smiled at him sidewise. "If Aubrey rages at me tomorrow, will you explain that you asked me to come and have a drink with you?"

He accepted the delicate proposal.

"You would like to have a drink?"

"Yes, please, Henry."

He summoned the waitress. Elena gave her order promptly. "Scotch on the rocks."

The waitress stared at her. "Say, did anyone ever tell you that you look like Elena Lonigan?"

"Yes," she said. "Lots of times."

"Well, it's true."

They laughed together, she and Henry, and he realized that he had not laughed for a long time. Then he was serious.

"I hope you don't drink often."

She fluttered her eyelashes at him. "Oh no! I couldn't. My second husband was an alcoholic. That's why I divorced him. Let me tell you something, Henry. They never get cured. They always go back to it. Come a little trouble and they're soaking it up again. I did everything for him. The money I spent on him—sanitariums and things! I'd try anything anybody told me. No use. I'd come home and there he'd be drunk as a lord. Do lords really drink? I've always wondered."

"I don't know. How long ago was that?"

"I've been alone a year. I guess Aubrey is counting on that, too. It's hard for a girl to be alone. I've never wanted to live with a girl. It's repulsive. I'm a man's woman."

Henry Potter coughed. "I hope you don't mean that he would take advantage of your lonely position."

"That would be up to me. Whether I wanted it

enough. No, it's just that he'll play a game with me, if you know what I mean—"

"I'm afraid I don't."

"Well—"

She bit her lip and looked away. "I don't know why I'm saying all this. I don't really know him too well. I'd like to know him better. Well, it's part of his meanness—or cleverness." She went on. "He tantalizes me, gets me to liking him, and then he plays the cold and dignified. He's cold at the bottom—or maybe he's got somebody. But he'll let me get myself crazy about him, so that I'll be a better actress, get my emotions stirred up, and then use them for the play. That's the method."

"What?"

"Oh, sure," she said. "Clay in the potter's hand, as the poets say. And I'm dumb enough to fall for it. Oh, there's some truth in it! I have to be a little crazy about the director if I'm to do my best—*willing* clay, you know? I have to *let* myself be molded. I have to *give*—"

She shook her head and sighed. "Over and over and over—they're all the same. But Aubrey has style. He makes you feel he's above the rest of them. Damn him —he *does* have style! He's a charmer—when he wants to use charm. Then, when you think he really means it, he lets you know—"

She broke off, biting her full lower lip.

"Know what?" Henry Potter asked.

"That you have to do what he tells you to do—to the last little movement, the last little word, or smile, or—whatever."

The waitress brought the Scotch, and Elena sipped it. "That's good, Henry. It warms me to the bottom.

My little seat was cold, there on the steps. I don't drink very often—honest, I don't!"

Henry Potter frowned. "If what you tell me about Dane is true—"

"It's true," she said. "And if he heard me tell you, he'd say why not? Anything for the show!"

He opened his mouth and she put out her hand.

"Wait—don't blame him! He won't ask me to sleep with him—right away, that is. Some of them do, but he won't. He'll just be hurt when I can't stand the frustration. He'll talk about loyalty and friendship and counting on me and how great the show will be if we work together. He'll be so damned honorable that I'll cry at night in bed and then work my fool head off for him all day. Now and then he'll call me 'darling' and 'sweetheart,' he'll give me a kiss on the cheek, hug me just enough to keep me going strong for him. And after the opening night I'll never see him again, except if it's a hit he'll stroll by to look at the show once in a while, and tell me how great I am, but that I'm slipping a little in the second act."

Henry Potter listened to this with indignation. "Are you in love with him?" he asked after a moment of silence.

She drank the rest of the Scotch in a gulp and set down the empty glass. "No, I'm not in love with him, but I shall be temporarily, at least—by the time we get into rehearsal. I know my own self. I'm an actress, see? I fall in love the way a baby falls into the bathtub if you don't watch it. And when I fall I drown. I can't help it. And that goddamn Aubrey Dane knows it. He counts on it, I tell you! Oh, he's got the worst reputation for meanness in the whole business—"

"You're not saying you want him to sleep with you!"

"Not while I'm in my right mind! But I won't be

in my right mind a few weeks from now. That's the way it affects me."

"What affects you?"

"Working on a part."

The steak came and his cup of tea. She began to eat quickly but daintily. He leaned on the table, arms folded, watching her face, and marveled at her, the lack of inhibition, the childlike frankness, the sweetness of her voice, the artlessness of her manner. He had never seen anyone like her. . . .

She looked up and met his eyes. "I don't know why I'm telling you all this," she said pleadingly. "I feel as though you were my father. . . ."

He felt a strange pang somewhere in his being. "I'm old enough to be—but I'm not."

"Oh, I don't feel you're old," she said. "It's just good to talk, now while I'm still myself. I hope I can talk with you once in a while, when we get into rehearsal. Maybe it'll help to keep me steady. I don't want to get crazy about Aubrey—or anybody. I want to do my work. I want to be a great actress—the greatest. And when I'm crazy about a man I can't do good work. That's what Aubrey can't understand. I'm not my best when I'm in love. Maybe I would be if I didn't know he was leading me on for his own purpose—as cold as a fish in the sea. . . . Henry, you don't think he's one of those, do you?"

He was startled by the question, but she answered herself.

"No, he's not. He couldn't charm women the way he does if he were. . . . I suppose he told you he was an orphan and all that?"

"He told me."

"He's no orphan! He's probably the son of a preacher —or an actor. I'll bet he's married to some jealous

female. He's crazy about her, though, or she couldn't
hold him away from other women the way she does."

"You think he lies?"

"It's just that I don't believe anybody."

"Are you sure you don't love him?"

"I'm afraid of him . . . so I don't love him. . . . But
I can't answer for myself when we get into rehearsal
and he stands there for hours, watching me, telling
me what to do, willing me to do what he wants me
to do. It's hypnosis. I keep thinking about it—dreading
it, but wanting it! That's part of being an actress. You
give yourself up. You *want* to be directed. You want
to be told—that is, if you have a good director. And
face it—Aubrey Dane is the best. You *want* him to
direct you—and he knows that. And he does it. And
he's always right. That's his—genius, I suppose you'd
call it."

He felt the chill of her dread and her longing. What
was this he was getting into?

The door opened and Aubrey Dane came in. He
saw them and walked to them swiftly.

"Elena, why didn't you wait for me?"

She looked up at him. "I did wait. And I was freez-
ing cold and Henry—Mr. Potter—told me to come
and have a drink with him. He said he'd explain to you
tomorrow."

"There's nothing to explain. You should have
waited!"

"And I waited," she said doggedly.

"Well, now you can go home and go to bed and
get some sleep. I'm calling the cast together tomorrow at ten o'clock and you'll be late. If you are late,
you'll be fired. That's my rule. You're not the queen.
Everybody's got to be there on time or get fired."

"Let her finish her steak," Henry Potter said.

Their eyes met and Aubrey Dane yielded. "All right, finish your steak, Elena. But from now on remember it's I who give the orders."

He went to another table and sat moody and alone. And Elena finished the steak quickly without another word and slipped into her coat. "Goodnight, Henry," she said in a whisper.

In the nearly empty restaurant Henry Potter sat drinking his tea and waiting for Aubrey Dane to come to him. After some fifteen minutes of such waiting he realized that Dane was not coming. The young man sat hunched over the table, gulping down coffee. Henry Potter rose, dropped some change on the table, put on his coat and left. His car was at the curb and Beaman was awake. When he saw his employer he got out briskly, touched his cap, opened the door in the manner of the best chauffeurs, and a moment later drove the big car silently home.

No sooner had Henry Potter entered his own house, however, than he heard the telephone ring. He took up the receiver and heard Aubrey Dane's voice, calm and charming.

"You got away without my seeing you, Henry. I hope it wasn't a guilty conscience. I must ask you not to talk with my cast, especially with Elena. If you have a comment to make, make it through me—otherwise there'll be total confusion."

He was instantly outraged. "What are you talking about, Dane? I wasn't having a private conference with anybody! The girl was sitting on the stairs, half frozen, waiting for you, and in simple kindness—"

"I daresay she complained of my cruelty and general wickedness, didn't she, and—"

"She did, and—"

"I thought so. The combat has begun! You're too

new at the business to realize that every actor is a child, especially if she's the star. She is compelled to hate me. I'm a father figure, a potential lover, the center of her emotions—temporarily. The truth is, she has no emotions—no permanent ones, that is—and she has to manufacture them fresh for every play. Our play demands a lot of emotion—hatred against an older husband, passion for a young lover. And Elena's empty. She knows it, and so she's beginning to foment and froth and cook up a brew of tumult inside herself."

"She was sitting on the stairs, shivering, and—"

"Who told her to sit on the stairs? Why didn't she come into the theater where I was? No, she was sitting there in a dramatic pose, waiting for me to come out and discover her. Do you think I didn't know she was there? Of course I did! And I would have let her sit there all night. I'd have left by another exit, I assure you, because I'm too intelligent and too experienced to be caught in such a trap. Never trust an actress! She's always acting—if she's good, and Elena's damned good."

Henry Potter pondered a reply and could think of none. It sickened him to believe that he had been made of a fool of, and he refused to believe it.

"Are you there?" Dane demanded.

"I'm here all right," he replied. "I don't know what to say. I don't know such people. Now I come to think of it, I don't even know people like you. You're a strange breed. I wonder how I ever got into this."

Dane's laughter came rippling over the wires. "Cheer up! You've a lot to learn, and you'll enjoy it. Goodnight, Henry! We begin rehearsals tomorrow. You'd better just stay away until I have the cast set."

Silence settled over the house. He went upstairs to his rooms and took a hot bath and climbed into bed. And lying there alone in the house, he thought of Ethel and wondered where she was, and was glad she was not here. He had begun something and he wished that he had not, and were she here he could not have restrained himself from telling her everything. And he had no intention of telling anybody anything. Some ancestral bullheadedness in him made him want to finish what he had begun. He went to sleep.

3

The next morning he returned to his own offices and to Marie. She asked no questions, although he discerned immeasurable question in her voice and every movement, in the sullenness of her demeanor, and he made himself busy. Privately he was somewhat disconcerted to discover how well his manifold business had done without him. He summoned his executives, heard their reports, and gave a few orders. The general atmosphere was that of his return from an unexplained illness, from which he had now recovered. The warmth of their reception was pleasant, and he resisted an inner doubt of himself. What had come over him that night to persuade him that comfort and security were dull? He toyed with the possibility that he would let Aubrey Dane run the show, and he himself would write off the money as a loss and appear no more in the dim and drafty hall where upon a bare stage a motley crowd of ill-dressed actors wandered about in disorder. These smartly dressed, clean-shaven young men, gathered in his office on a bright morning, their eyes alert and confident, smiling at him, compelled response.

"Well, gentlemen," he said. "What's the report?"

"Last month's sales showed an all-time high, sir," his general manager said. Good man, this Dan Berger, Harvard graduate of six years ago, neatly dressed in a dark business suit, married to a millionaire's daughter but not living extravagantly, father of a girl and boy, and generally liked. "Not only for us," he continued, "but all over the country. What's good for the country is good for us, don't you think, sir? And our last six months are better than any time since 1967—"

The accustomed routines, the long traveled paths of his business went on as before. He had not been missed. A vague gloom crept over his spirit. He was dispensable, but he listened, approved, and sent them back to their offices. He had made it a practice to keep himself surrounded by young men. Was it a mistake? Against their shining assurance, their self-confidence, their security, he felt himself old beyond his years. At one o'clock he went upstairs to his private dining room and ate his luncheon alone. Sweetbreads! He detested them.

"Doesn't the chef know better than to serve me sweetbreads?" he demanded of the company butler.

"He's new, sir," the butler replied. "Biggers got a job in a hotel, sir. He said he wanted more excitement."

"*You* know I don't like sweetbreads."

"It escaped my mind, sir. You haven't had your luncheon here for some time, sir."

"Don't let it happen again!"

"No, sir."

He ate the sweetbreads gloomily and, returning to his office, felt singularly unemployed. At half past two he rose and put on his hat and coat. He was under no contract to obey Aubrey Dane. He had merely put money into a new business, and he had every right to look after his money. He told Marie to tell Beaman he would make his own way home and, taking a taxicab, he arrived at the theater, amazed to feel his heart beating perceptibly faster, whether from fear of Aubrey

Dane, or from another reason, remained to be discovered.

Inside the theater, dim except for the brazen light upon the bare stage, there was silence and the air of absorption. Aubrey Dane and Chess Bates were making chalk marks on the stage, and a few actors strolled about. The child actors played dominoes quietly in another corner, and some women who, he supposed, were their mothers, watched from the front row. He sat alone in the shadows, and ruminated while Dane worked, speaking now and again in a low voice, ignoring everyone except Chess. Then he grew impatient and strolled to the stage.

"What are you fellows doing—getting ready to play hopscotch?" he called.

"Call it that," Dane said. He dusted the chalk from his hands. "We're just marking out preliminary positions."

"Meaning—"

"The actors have to know exactly where to stand."

"You mean they don't stand as they please, walk around—"

"Certainly not," Dane said. "They have to be told everything—down to the last clinch! That's my job."

"They're mannikins?"

"In a way, yes. Again, not—"

Dane sauntered down into the dim theater with him and they sat down in the front row of empty seats. He lit a cigarette. Henry Potter glanced at the glowing end.

"You aren't supposed to smoke in here, are you?"

"Have to," Dane said. "I couldn't stand the gaff if I didn't. Sure, it's against the fire rules. Inspector comes around once in a while but the word goes ahead.

We put the cigarettes in our pockets until he's gone. He knows, of course, but as long as he doesn't see—"

"The slogan of our age," Henry Potter observed.

"Maybe it is," Dane conceded, "but if so, it's because we have an impossible number of rules, regulations, laws—we're too damned idealistic for our own good!"

"Let people burn themselves up, you mean?"

"Exactly." Henry Potter returned to his curiosity. "In what way aren't these people mannikins, if they have to wait for you to tell them where to stand, where to sit, what to say—"

"Even what to think and what to feel," Dane said. "But they have to have the capability, once they're told. That's what makes them actors—the incapability of doing anything until they're told what to do and how to do it, and then the capability."

"You revolt me," Henry Potter said drily. "You're a hypnotist, a dictator, a tyrant!"

Dane sat up. "Look, if you let a lot of actors act without direction you'd have no play. A play is a cooperative creation. You're handed the shape by the writer, but that shape has to be brought to life in flesh and blood, and that flesh and blood means certain people who have to be told how to do what they have to do, or it would never get done. They *want* to be told—they know they can't do anything without being told. But if they have the direction they can do it."

"Who directs you?"

"I'm not an actor," Dane retorted. "A good director is never a good actor—and the other way around. Or so I believe—"

He paused to light another cigarette, then went on talking, the cigarette hanging on his lower lip.

"Look—it oughtn't to be hard for you to understand! You're the one who directs your business, aren't you? You've taught and trained, you supervise, you give the orders, you bring everything together into a whole. Well, that's what I do, in my own way."

They heard high heels tripping down the aisle and looking up they saw Elena approach and pause.

"Aubrey?"

"Yes, darling—"

Darling! Henry Potter was startled. What was this?

"Aubrey, I need help with my part."

"Sure—in your dressing room."

Dane rose and walked down the aisle with his arm about her shoulders. It was two hours before they came back. Henry Potter sat patiently waiting. The stage had filled with waiting actors. The grim white light poured down on them from the huge naked bulb which dangled on a cord high above their heads. He continued to wait, imagining dark goings-on in that dressing room.

On the stage the actors waited in static patience, as though for fate. Now and then someone rose to flex muscles or go to the toilet. One man rose every fifteen minutes and stood on his head in the corner and returned, refreshed, to sit down again on his rickety chair. Chess Bates was busy marking and erasing the dusty floor. Once when he approached the edge of the stage Henry Potter was compelled to rise and walk down the sloping aisle and make a demand.

"Where's Dane?"

"Working with Elena," Chess Bates said absently.

"Tell him I'm going to my office."

"All right."

At that moment Dane appeared briskly, and with him Elena. She had brushed her hair into a shining aureole and her lips were scarlet. She had a demure look and her smile upon the cast was vivid. They did not respond. They looked at her blankly, as though they had never seen her before, but they made way for her and she took her seat in the center of a semicircle. Chess Bates had found a small unpainted table, and a kitchen stool, and a barrel. Dane sat upon the stool by the table and Chess sat on the barrel.

At this moment Dane turned his head. "Come up here, Mr. Potter," he called. "I want the cast to meet you."

He walked up the aisle, conscious of a blush of shyness, and stood hesitating at the foot of the steps.

"Come up," Dane urged. "We can't see you down there."

He climbed the three rickety steps and, except for Elena, he faced as motley a crowd of human beings as he had ever seen. They were extraordinarily plain of face. Where had Dane picked up such a crew? The girls were of indeterminate age without makeup, their skins dingy, hair unkempt. The men were no better, unshaven, unbathed, he guessed. Not one of them spoke to him. What material was this?

"Mr. Henry Potter," Dane was saying. "Industrialist, capitalist, but to us—the producer, the fellow that puts up the dough."

They stared at him with dull eyes and certainly without interest and not one spoke to him. He was not inclined to speak to them, either, and he stood awkwardly, wishing he had remained in the safe dimness of the empty theater.

"Sit down, Henry," Dane said carelessly. "Sit down there in the front row."

He climbed down the rickety steps again and sat down and looked up at the group. Aubrey was in command. It was not merely that only he assumed command, it was also that command was thrust upon him. Each of these silent drab beings subdued itself to the dominant standing figure. Each yearned to yield. Their bodies inclined toward Dane, their faces were upturned to him unconsciously, he would have said, except that he felt vaguely that not one movement these creatures made was unconscious or even instinctive. They were detached, in a curious way careless of themselves, and yet profoundly self-centered, like children—yes, that was it. They were self-centered in the way that children are, absorbed in their bodily functions. Someone belched and they laughed suddenly, like children.

Aubrey Dane was talking in a firm, steady monotone.

"We have a very difficult play to create. It says things that people don't want to hear said. It will make people think, and people hate to think. So don't imagine you have an easy job ahead. You'll have to work. Even with four weeks of rehearsal we haven't enough time. We'll go out of town for two weeks. That makes six weeks. It's not time enough for this play. But it'll have to do, thanks to union pay scales. I don't believe it can possibly be a hit, but maybe it won't be a flop. We'll see. It depends on each one of you—and on me. I'm ruthless. I'll help anybody that wants help and I'll force it on anybody that doesn't. That'll do for today. We'll work every day including Sundays starting at eleven in the morning. If anybody is late he or she will be fired. There are plenty more where you came from."

To this announcement there was silence and then a tittering, nervous, subdued laughter.

Henry Potter listened with wondering indignation. Did Dane have to talk to them as though they were morons? He examined their faces to see signs of resentment. What he saw were relief and a dawning cheerfulness. For the first time he heard voices and an echo of laughter, when Dane dismissed them. They were children at play, dreaming themselves into creatures they were not and could never be, building a world as shifting and glimmering as a rainbow. He got up quickly and left the theater.

His life now assumed a new pattern. He rose early, breakfasted alone in the sunny breakfast room to the east of the dining room, a small cheerful octagon of a room, designed by Ethel to catch the morning sun. She was an early riser and never breakfasted in bed. He could hear her verdict: "A messy habit!"

By his plate today was her letter. She wrote daily, and mailed the accumulation once a week or as nearly that as she could manage on the cruise schedule. Her letters were invariably cheerful.

"I can imagine you at breakfast, dear," she wrote. "You are in the breakfast room. Let's see. It's February. It may not be sunny. It's hard to imagine no sun—I'm drenched in the sun here on the top deck. We're cruising among the islands—lovely green against a purple-blue sky. The very sky is different here. Oh, Henry dear, I do so wish you had come with me! It's impossible to describe the tropics' beauty. One has to see—and feel."

See and feel! That was Ethel. She saw and felt everything—everybody—except the man who was her husband. Toward him she maintained her silvery sweetness, tolerant, seeming to understand—or at least to accept—everything.

"She'd never understand——" he muttered over his scrambled eggs and bacon.

Well, his conscience reminded him, did he even understand himself? What quixotic, do-good impulse had persuaded him to this adventure? His morning hours he spent in his office seemingly as usual, but promptly after an early luncheon, he went to the theater, leaving Marie looking at him doubtfully. He read her simple mind and ignored it. She supposed, faithful and troubled, that he was carrying on an affair with some damned female while his wife was away.

He rose now, chuckling to himself, and in the hall Nora waited with his hat and topcoat.

"Home for dinner, sir?"

"I'll let you know," he replied.

That was another lesson he was learning. He never knew whether Dane would want to stay at the theater for talk or for an hour or two, or three, with an actor, and suggest that he stay, too.

"I want you to share in this, Mr. Potter," he said. "We're partners, pro tem."

Only the sessions with Elena were private. She seemed now to live only when she was with Dane. She walked in a daze, heard only his voice, was, in fact, his creature. He dominated—no, he possessed her, a demonic possession, it seemed. He was ruthless and she was his subject.

Again he went to his office, worked doggedly at his desk through the morning, ate a sandwich Marie brought him from the luncheon room, and, ignoring her troubled look, he left and went to the theater.

Day after day he returned to sit in the darkened theater, alone, the empty seats haunted by people who were not there. Upon the stage, isolated under the glare of the lights, Dane worked almost in silence with one and another of the marionettes, who were the actors—children, he called them, his children—

cutting deep into himself and into them, carving into them the groove of dependence upon his will, the rut of subservience to his need to dominate them and from them to create his own work of art and yet in most subtle fashion leading them, persuading, coaxing them to exercise to the utmost the reach of their own talent.

Though how could he penetrate that untried material, Henry Potter wondered, and see the spark of talent that burned within? The actors were dressed anyhow, old slacks and dirty sweaters, feet sandaled or bare, hair tousled. At first they had all looked alike but he was beginning now to see that they were not alike. Then to his own amazement he began to see in them not the frowsy people he had seen at first but the characters in the play, the older scientist, the young physicist, the wife—and he perceived that Aubrey Dane was re-creating these men and women. He was fixing them in new personalities. The people in the play were emerging under his skillful direction.

Elena was apart, always apart, and waiting her turn when to her alone Aubrey Dane would direct his entire attention. She held herself aloof, refusing anything but the whole of him. She lay flat on the floor, legs outstretched. Usually she wore long tight knit trousers shaped so close to her thin frame that her rounded mound of Venus protruded, ostentatiously obvious. This sight Henry Potter had always avoided, attracted and repelled, but he had watched the other men, even Dane himself, and had perceived, cynically, that under their ostensible ignoring of her, they were acutely and sexually aware of her. A dirty business!

This morning, however, when he seated himself in his usual seat in the front row of empty seats in the theater, Henry Potter saw that Elena had come in wearing a short brown corduroy skirt and a sleeveless red blouse. Her hair hung as usual unbrushed, uncombed, over her forehead. As usual, he realized, her presence dominated the stage. The entire cast was there, and Aubrey Dane was rehearsing a scene between the two scientists while Elena waited. She sat on the floor in center stage, her bare legs curled under her, as she watched Dane intently. The other actors had grouped themselves about her, without intent probably, and yet drawn toward her as she assumed, day after day, the central role in the drama.

Henry Potter watched her, fascinated and puzzled. They were all watching her, he knew, and as she knew, for she, too, was assuming the place of the star. She had ceased to be herself, a puzzled, half-frightened shabby girl, and instead was becoming the poised and even dominating star. Now as he gazed at her, fascinated and wondering, suddenly she sat up to hug her knees. From where Henry Potter sat it was impossible not to see that she wore nothing under the skirt. He blushed, looked away, then looked again and was angry that he blushed. He told himself that she was as careless as a naked child, but, he thought sternly, she was not a child! She was a woman and, he did not doubt, completely knowing of what she did. Her white thighs, the dark shadow between, were revealed in simple wantonness. Dane, his eyes upon her, did not hesitate or falter in his directing of the group.

"Children," he was saying in his low, softly modulated voice. "Children, this is what I want you to do! Remember the Englishman has just come into the room. You do not know why he has come. Elena, you were once in love with him, years ago when your roads crossed, but you put him out of your mind. Now when you see him you know that he has always been in your mind and still is."

She listened, her face uplifted, her knees drawing apart. If Dane saw what she meant him to see, he gave no sign. He kept talking to her, gazing at her, directing her. There was a current between them, and every actor was aware of it.

Henry Potter could bear no more. He rose and walked to the seats in the back of the theater. They were raised enough so that he looked down upon the platform. What people were these? Who was this woman? And above all what was he doing here?

Dane glanced over his shoulder and turned again to the cast. "Now, children," he said, "let's take the last scene over again."

Elena jumped lightly to her feet. Tension subsided.

At five o'clock Dane dismissed them. "Break until seven o'clock. We'll do a run-through of the first act tonight." He leaped from the platform and strode up the aisle.

"Your wife back, Henry?" Temporarily, Dane had arrived at his first name. No one else had ever done so, except of course Ethel. He was not a man who encouraged the use of his first name, but Dane somehow—

"No," he said curtly.

"Then I wish you'd take Elena to dinner. She expects me to do it every night, damn her, but I need the time for business tonight. A lot of contracts yet to be signed—Equity stuff. I wonder sometimes how we ever get a show on."

"I don't want to take her to dinner," he said shortly. "I wouldn't know what to say to her."

"Oh, come now," Dane said. "You talked that night. You picked her up from the stairs. Besides, you needn't say anything. She'll talk your head off—about herself, of course. That's all she knows, all she thinks about. And she has a crush on you, believe it or not. She pretends to be tired of young men. She's been asking me why you don't take her to dinner. Producers do, you know—it's part of the ritual. Star expects it. Hold her hand, there's a good fellow. I get tired of doing it."

"I wouldn't know how," he muttered.

"She'll help you," Dane said.

A man came up with papers and a pen. "Mr. Dane, please—the contracts—you and Mr. Potter both sign."

They signed, and before he could slip away Elena herself was walking toward them, her bare feet in scarlet slippers.

"Sweetheart," Dane said, "Henry is taking you to dinner."

"Oh, lovely," she cried softly, "I've been wanting that."

"So go off," Dane said, "and leave me to my chores." He hurried away.

Henry Potter stared down upon Elena's pale face and did not meet her eyes.

"Where do you want to eat?" he grunted.

"How about that nice place next door?" she said almost slyly but not quite. Again she tucked her hand into his elbow, a not quite clean hand, he noticed, and they walked outside. He was glad he had sent Beaman away. So far as he could see, there was no one who could possibly know him. She had not combed her hair, her face was without makeup, and she looked no more than fifteen, he thought uncomfortably. No one must see this!

They entered the restaurant, a dim, Italian place

and a waiter sidled up to Elena. "Your usual table, Elena?"

"Yes, Paolo," she said.

They strolled, her hand still in his arm and he still uncomfortable, to a distant table, half hidden in shadows. She slid into the corner seat and leaned her wan cheek on her hand.

"Why does a waiter call you Elena?" he demanded.

She studied the menu and did not lift her eyes. "Why not? It's my name."

"Your personal name, not for waiters!"

"In the theater people don't have last names," she said indifferently. She pointed a thin forefinger upon the menu.

"Filet mignon—very rare, please, Henry, Persian melon, black coffee."

Henry Potter gave the order for their food and the waiter smiled mysteriously and went away.

"I have to go to the bathroom, Henry."

"Very well," he said, only why did he have to know?

She rose and sauntered off and people turned their heads to watch her move, graceful as an eel, between the tables. He sat, waiting and thoughtful. What breed of human being was this among whom by what chance he had fallen? He had a sudden longing for Ethel, for her clean good looks, her healthy calm. But he would see this through, he thought doggedly. It was a kind of life, underground life, seldom in the sunshine, lived in the murky depths of dank and empty theaters and wretched boarding houses. And yet out of mud, he had heard it said in India, there may bloom a lotus. He would see.

She was back almost before he had finished brooding upon his metaphor, and she sighed as she slid into her seat.

"Boy, but I feel better! I try to remember to go to the bathroom the last thing before I'm onstage, but sometimes I forget and then I suffer—boy, do I suffer —especially if I have to play the big love scene."

"I can imagine," Henry Potter said drily.

She smiled at him, a suddenly sweet movement of the lips and a glimmer in the dark eyes. "Can you imagine? Really? The relief, you know—as if suddenly you were able to breathe—"

"It's a common experience, I assure you," he said, "especially in early childhood."

She pouted full red lips. "Are you laughing at me, Henry?"

"Not exactly."

"But a little?"

"Here's your steak."

The waiter uncovered the silver dish and moved browned meat tenderly to her plate. Upon it he heaped the mushrooms. Then he held out a menu.

"Would you autograph it, Elena? I seen you in every pitcher. You're my favorite."

She smiled up at him, dark eyes melting, and scrawled her name across the list of desserts. He laughed quick Italian laughter.

"Right where you belong—thanks, Elena. Yours'll be done in a minute, mister."

He went away and she cut her meat into strips, dripping blood.

"I begged Tootles to fix it so you'd ask me to dinner," she said.

"Tootles?"

"That's my pet name for Aubrey. I always call my directors Tootles."

She was lying, of course. Or perhaps Dane was lying. They all lied, he had discovered, and as easily as they breathed. It had been a shock to know this, accustomed as he was to the comparative integrity of his peers, but he perceived that, like children, they believed what they said when they said it.

"It's my pleasure," he replied.

"You say that so nicely," she murmured, and looked at him pleadingly. "Henry, I want you to know I'm not happy in the play."

"No? Why not? I thought it was a good play."

"It's all right, I suppose," she said grudgingly. "Only who's the playwright? As I said to Tootles, I don't want to be caught in a play by someone I never heard of. Suppose it's a flop! I can't afford that. I have movie contracts."

"I suppose I should say it can't be a flop with you in it, shouldn't I?"

"You're sweet." She put out her hand and he found himself clasping it unwillingly. It was hot and dry, a handful of little bones. He let it go, but she clung.

"You have a nice hand, Henry—strong and cool! That's what I need—somebody strong and cool. I'm not happy, Henry—I'm not happy in the play. And my love life—well, I haven't any. Of course there's Tootles—"

"Tootles?"

"I could fall in love with him, of course, and he expects it, but I'm not sure it's worthwhile if the play's going to be a flop—"

He subdued a gasp. "He expects you to—"

"Oh, sure," she said, chewing daintily between words, "I told you how that is. It makes it easier for him if I do—I'm always wax when I fall in love. Hypnotized, almost! Still, it's wearing after a while, when you're a professional—"

"Professional what, in God's name?"

"Don't swear, Henry. Professional actress, that's all."

"But you don't mean you have to fall in love with every goddamn—"

"Henry, please don't swear! My mother taught me not to and I don't like to hear it even though I do it myself sometimes. Like I said, love helps. When you're crazy about a guy naturally you do your best for him. It would be easy enough for me to fall for Tootles— he's got magnetism. But I don't know. I'd like security for a change. Maybe I ought to get married again."

He felt a warm discomfort. Was he not a bulwark of security? She was looking at him thoughtfully as she ate.

"I've had a terrible life, Henry," she moaned, shaking her tousled head. "I come of nice people, too— would you believe it?"

"I can believe it," he said.

There was something rather touching about her face, small and pale under that mop of dark gold hair.

"Tell me about yourself," he said when she fell silent.

It was what she wanted, of course, and he found himself doing what she wanted, she meanwhile eating her meat as daintily voracious as a young cat at work on a plump mouse. She ate as she talked.

"My father was a salesman—handsome and terribly attractive to women—dark and tall and straight and he had a lovely deep, soft voice. His voice even sent goose shivers up and down my spine and when I was only twelve years old—he was something like Tootles. My mother was English and sweet and sad, poor thing, because of course women couldn't and wouldn't let my father alone. You're handsome, too, Henry—did you know? In a quiet, big sort of way—I could fall for you, too!"

She was not coquettish—merely thoughtful as she looked him over.

"Let's not talk about me," he growled.

She laughed and put out the hot impulsive little hand again. He looked at it and did not move.

"No?" Her voice was inquiring, softly inquiring.

"No," he said, as though he were declining a bargain.

She withdrew the hand and sighed. "Well, as I say, I loved my father and I felt sorry for my mother, especially when I began to grow up—I was about fourteen, I think. No, I was exactly fourteen, on my birthday, I remember, when my father looked at me like he'd never seen me before. I was pouring his breakfast coffee, leaning over, not thinking, and suddenly I felt his hand under my left breast. I guess I had a low neckline or something."

She put her hand beneath her left breast under her thin blouse and lifted it as though she were offering its smooth firmness to him.

"Good God," he muttered, and looked about.

"Don't interrupt, Henry, and don't look at me like a scared old fuddy-duddy. Just *listen,* please, like a good boy. . . ."

"Now, look here, Elena," Henry declared sternly. Who was this girl-woman sitting across from him, he asked himself, who dared to call *him,* Henry Potter, an old fuddy-duddy *and* a good boy? He was uncomfortable while she made him blush. . . .

"Good God," he muttered again. "Where's that damned waiter?"

"Coming, sir!"

The man appeared and with a flourish of lid and cutlery served his steak.

"That about right, sir?"

"Yes—it's been long enough," Henry said shortly.

"Perfection takes time, sir," the waiter said briskly. He smiled down at Elena.

"How'd you like a nice hot roll, Elena?"

She shook her head. "Can't risk a pound now, Paolo!"

He went away and she lifted her dark eyelashes. "Poor dear Henry, I'm embarrassing you. You really don't want me to go on?"

"No!"

And then, impelled by a curiosity which he could not understand, he burst out again.

"Are those eyelashes your own?"

She laughed. "Why, Henry, how sweet of you to notice! Yes, they're my own. I mean, natural. They're my one real vanity. Why do you ask?"

"I remember—" he blurted and then stopped.

He remembered the first evening that Ethel had put on false eyelashes. Yes, they were going to the theater—some play he'd forgotten. He had stared at her, amazed.

"You're not putting on those damn—"

She had laughed. "Yes, I am, Henry! I've always wanted long eyelashes and mine are short. But now I can buy them, and they're the style, so why not?"

He had been silent and stared at her. His own wife —and now this little slut, this Elena, and her long eyelashes were real! There was no justice—

Elena interrupted his thoughts. "Why don't you say something, Henry, instead of just sitting there staring at me? No, no, don't say anything. Just listen, because I want to tell you, Henry—I need to tell you. Because I grew up in that second. I *knew*, Henry. Suddenly I knew everything—about sex, about men and women. Oh, I've learned the details since, of course, all of them, I guess, but that day I *knew*. I loved my father—and when he put his hand under my breast, suddenly I loved him not just as my father, but as a man. Henry, I *knew* what he was doing, and I wanted him to do it. I wanted him to do *everything!* I told him I knew he had lots of women and I wanted him to love me as a woman, not a little girl. It wasn't exactly his fault because women are so damned bitchy. Henry, you know they are. I am, too. Why, if I wanted to be as bitchy as I know how to be, I could even get you in love with me."

"Let's not dwell on that," Henry mumbled.

"I remember he pressed me to him," Elena continued, "and he began kissing me on the mouth, my arms, my neck, and then he put his hands up under my skirt and was surprised to find out I wasn't wearing any panties. I never do, even now."

"Obviously," Henry commented wryly, remembering the short brown corduroy skirt.

"You're interrupting," Elena said sharply. "Anyway, that was the beginning, Henry—the beginning of sex between my father and me—between a man and me. I wasn't ashamed, and neither was he, I don't think. It seemed all right, I mean, we loved each other. He was gentle and sure of himself. He petted me and stroked me and said he didn't want to hurt me. And he didn't, Henry, he didn't. He came to my bed late at night when my poor mother was sound asleep, and sometimes he made love to me right in the kitchen— and I liked it—I loved it! But I knew, as young as I was, that my mother would be hurt and, well, somehow I couldn't stay home. I stayed there for a few weeks. I locked my bedroom door, I tried—but—"

He broke in again. "All right, where did you go?"

"I came to live with my aunt here in New York. She always wanted me, since her husband died, and I guess Mother knew my father, because she'd never let me leave home before and suddenly she did. Once I was here, it was easy enough to do as I pleased. Aunt Angela was such a saint. It was terribly easy to fool her. Of course she didn't want me to be an actress, but I said I must and so she said very well, and sent me to the school for children who want to act. I got a job when I was sixteen. My aunt died last year. . . . Henry, are you listening?"

"Yes—sort of—"

He was not listening. He was imagining her firm little breast, so young, in his hand.

She stabbed at a mushroom and conveyed it to her mouth.

"Henry—"

"Yes?"

"Could you help me about something?"

"I doubt it."

She put down her fork and leaned her elbows on the table and laced her fingers together under her chin. "Yes, you can. Please, please, don't let me fall in love with Aubrey Dane."

"Why not? If it helps you with your job—"

"I don't want to go through the agony again—in case I really love him."

"He might love you."

"Oh, no—he'll pretend, of course—just enough to stir up my emotions so that I can act well. I might sleep with him a few times—he'll want me to, if I don't fall quickly enough—but that'll be all. When the show opens, I'll never see him again. Henry—please!"

She was trembling, the little creature, and to his horror he saw great tears roll down her cheeks. He had never seen a woman cry in beauty. For that matter he had never seen any woman cry since Ethel's mother died, and certainly Ethel had not been beautiful then. Marie did not count. Tears always welled into her pale eyes if he lost his temper, and then her nose turned red.

"Here, take my handkerchief," he muttered.

She took it and buried her face in it. "It's so nice and b-big," she sobbed. "I do love a big handkerchief to cry in."

"Now finish your dinner," he said.

She lifted her face. "I can't, Henry, please— We could sit in the back of the theater."

He let her cling to him, both hands folded over his arm, and they went into the theater and sat far back. No one was there yet except the assistant director, a callow boy from Yale, arranging the chairs on the stage. In the dark Elena leaned her head against his shoulder and curled herself against him and whispered.

"Oh, Henry, it's divine to have someone I can trust— lovely and divine—"

What he might have said to this he did not know. For he was delivered. He looked around by instinct and saw across the aisle the white and startled face of his chauffeur.

"Beaman," he called distinctly, "take me home!"

"Instantly, sir," Beaman said.

He rose and Henry Potter followed, disengaging Elena in silence. Out in the street he got into his car and was driven away. Halfway home, pondering whether to speak, he was again relieved by Beaman.

"I hope you won't think I was nosy, sir. I just went in to wait for you. Fact is, I've been sitting in the back for several days now. I'm fond of the theater. It's been interesting to watch how the play is shaping up. Nicely, I should say, sir. Mr. Dane is very talented."

"Beaman," Henry Potter said, "I am glad you were there. It made me feel safe."

He spoke with feeling, but the reply was cool and colorless.

"Yes, sir. Thank you, sir."

Afterwards, waking in the deep of the night, it seemed to him that he could not have managed better to convey to his chauffeur that whatever he had seen was none of his, Henry Potter's doing. An actress is an actress. But he would not take Elena again to dinner alone. . . . And then as though through the darkness his caution had awakened her, the telephone rang at his bedside. When he reached for the receiver, he heard her voice.

"Henry?"

"Yes?"

"Are you mad at me?"

"Of course not."

"I'm at home, Henry—and I can't sleep."

"Try, there's a good girl."

"Henry, could I speak to your wife?"

"She's not here. Remember?"

"Where is she, Henry?"

"Cruising somewhere around South America."

"Oh—"

Oh, and what an actress, he thought. She had inquired as to his marital status and the whereabouts of his wife!

He heard her again. "Then why were you afraid when your chauffeur saw us? Because he might tell?"

"There's nothing to tell."

"No, I know that. Except—"

He let her pause without answer, and she went on quickly.

"Henry, please don't be cross with me. I'm so lonely.

You've no idea how lonely life can be for an actress. I'm never myself, you know. In fact, I don't know what myself is."

"I can't help you there."

"Only by letting me talk to you. . . . Please, Henry? You won't say no?"

"You'll be busy, too busy for talk. Two more weeks, two weeks out of town, and then the opening—"

"Why are you afraid of me, Henry?"

"I'm not," he said sharply. "It's just that—" His turn to pause now, and she took it up sweetly.

"I know, Henry. You're faithful to your wife. But I would be, too. It's just that I need a sort of father— so badly. And Tootles is really too young for that. He'll turn into a lover, if you're not my father. And I don't want another lover—truly I don't!"

"Well—strictly on those terms, I—"

"Strictly!" Her lovely voice came fervently over the wires. "Thank you, Henry. And goodnight—darling!"

He heard the click of the receiver set firmly into its nest and he groaned and got up to make himself a drink.

He rose late the next morning and went to his office and delayed by every means his return to the theater. The morning was translucent, the welcome thin sunshine splintered by brief cold winds, the sun hot against the stone walls of the skyscrapers, and between the buildings the blast of lingering winter caught him as he stepped from his car.

In the silence of his office he read contracts and reports and memoranda while Marie waited for him to summon her. The habits of his respectable and secure life assumed control, and for a few seconds at a time he all but forgot the dusty theater, the glaring stage, the antic human beings strutting there. Only for a few seconds, and then he remembered and always the point of memory was Elena. He dreaded to see her, fearing the clutch of her hands, the hands of a pleading child. A child and alone! Where did she live now that her aunt was dead? Impossible that she could return to her father!

He became aware at this moment of an uncomfortable stir somewhere in his physical being, an impulse to be aborted, a slight warmth quickening the beat of his heart. In a mild panic he pressed the buzzer to summon Marie. She came in, wearing the look of prudent withdrawal, a reproach she did not deign to express. She sat down across the desk from him and opened her pad.

"All right, Mr. Potter."

He began the usual rote of dictation. "Dear Sir: Yours of the ninth—"

For two hours he dictated, corrected sometimes by Marie's nasal interruption—"You said that already, Mr. Potter"—and at twelve he could no longer cope with his curiosity.

"That'll do for today, Marie. I'll be back tomorrow morning."

She rose, reluctant. "Where can I get you, Mr. Potter?"

He evaded her. "I'll call you in the middle of the afternoon."

"All right, Mr. Potter but you know there's a board meeting of Potter Subsidiaries."

"Let Lewis take my place. What are vice-presidents for?"

"You said last time that I was to remind you that—"

"Well, you have."

He grunted and left and Beaman drove him in silence

through the crowded streets. The traffic was a snarl and his thoughts outran the vehicle. He was late. Dane would have given the command for the hour-long break for lunch. She might not be there. When the car stopped in front of the theater he got out and strode into the empty shadows. Elena and Dane were sitting alone, side by side, in the middle of the central block. Dane had his arm around her. Standing there he saw her drop her head upon Dane's shoulder, and Dane leaned his cheek against her hair. It had begun! He turned in a pang of horrifying jealousy, thinking only of escape. Then, in anger, he sat down quietly in the back row and waited, watching.

Dane was talking to her in a low, secret voice. He was saying something to which she responded by lifting her head. She kissed his cheek gently and let her head rest again on his shoulder. His voice murmured on, hypnotic, serpentine, and altogether revolting. It was not to be endured. Henry Potter made a bark of a cough and Dane's voice ceased. For a second he was silent, immobile. Then he rose, easy and graceful, and looked around.

"Hello, Henry," he called. "When did you come in? Run along now, Elena, sweetheart. Get a bite of lunch and hurry back and we'll finish the scene."

"Do I have to eat all by myself?"

"All by yourself today, honey. I want to talk business with Henry."

He helped her with her jacket and then walked down the aisle ahead of her and sat down beside Henry Potter. Elena went out alone and without speaking and, Henry Potter imagined, without wanting to look at him. And this, after the sobbing pleas of yesterday, and no later than midnight, last night! He was stiff with renewed anger, speechless and hostile to this slender, graceful young man, this cool and calm young man, who made a business of tampering with the emotions of sex not for his own emotional satisfactions, but for business, for the success of the play, through the torment of a woman, a child, who wanted to be a star.

"I was talking over the first love scene with Elena," Dane said carelessly. "She has plenty of emotion but her imagination has to be roused. She's not a self-starter. What's the matter? Are you shocked, Henry?"

"Disgusted is the word," Henry Potter said slowly. "Revolted. Amazed. I'm beginning to see what a play costs in human terms."

Dane opened his shrewd dark eyes. They were small eyes, Henry Potter saw now for the first time, small and sharp, and Dane's voice changed from its pleasant softness to harsh command.

"Don't talk nonsense about something that's not your business, Henry. I'm responsible for the success of this play. You only put up the money. Anybody can put up money. But people expect something of me. They expect a success. I'm famous for success and I don't intend to have a failure on my hands just because I'm experimenting with a new kind of play. I'm responsible to the actors and to the—they have faith in me. I'm even responsible to you—so that you get your money back."

"Damn the money," Henry Potter said but Dane would not let him finish.

"I never damn money. It's a necessity. No money, no show."

"Do you have to paw a girl to have a success?"

Dane stared at him. "What are you talking about? How foul can you get? I'm married—and happily! I don't paw!"

"What were you doing then? Stroking her, getting her to kiss you—"

"Nonsense." Dane's voice was cold and reasoning. "Henry, I see I shall have to educate you. Elena is an actor. I'm not even saying she's an actress. Actor! For this I thank God. I can't make an actor. She was born what she is, the way Beethoven was born a musician, or Shakespeare a playwright—not genius, perhaps, but a talent. The talent is hidden inside her, dammed up, obstructed by all sorts of fears and lack of self-confidence. I have to clear away the clutter—the way you clean the bed of a brook so that the water can flow freely from the spring."

"Do you have to make her fall in love with you?"

Dane lit a cigarette. He drew hard and let the smoke escape gently from between his lips. "Perhaps I do, if there is no other way."

"A willing sacrifice!"

Dane laughed. "Don't act so righteous, Henry, for God's sake! I'd much prefer she didn't mix up love with her job—sex, rather—but if she does, it's the only way to make her believe in herself. I'll disengage myself the day after we open."

"And hurt her?"

"She won't be hurt, Henry. If she's a success, she'll forget all about me in five minutes because she'll have herself to be in love with, and she's her own first love and last love and all the love between. That's why she's a great actress. . . .

"You don't believe me? Look here, Henry, I wouldn't dare let myself fall in love with an actress! It would be offering myself to be burnt alive in my own fire because she couldn't love anybody except herself—a whirl at sex, yes, she can make that any time. But love? No. In self-protection I couldn't and wouldn't let her think it possible."

"Your modern distinctions sicken me," Henry said.

"They're as modern as Adam and Eve."

Dane rose, restless to be at work. He went to the stage and Henry Potter sat watching in confused silence. The cast was coming in, one by one, the children gamboling like lambs beside their mothers. Children of the theater, children of the night! When did they play? When did they go to school? He saw them working at school books five minutes at a time, an hour or so throughout the day, their mothers scolding, persuading, and as alert as they to the call from the stage.

"Children, onstage!"

"Quick—they're calling you—"

Books were dropped, lessons forgotten, and they ran to the stage to take up their real life, parroting the words put into their mouths, learning to dance, to laugh in false gaiety when the director commanded mirth. If their mothers left them they hid among the seats, playing small quiet games of their own, emerging to make transient friendship with anyone who happened to be near.

Thus, in the next hour after luncheon, the child, Mary Jane, skipped down the aisle and stopped at Henry Potter's side, while Dane was rehearsing with Elena and Bert, the young male lead. She sat down in the seat next to him and smoothed down her short skirt.

"Are you Elena's father?"

"Most certainly not, I'm Mr. Henry Potter."

"Why are you here, Mr. Potter?"

"It's my show."

"You mean you're the backer?"

"Exactly."

God, what sad, worldly wisdom! This scrap of female wisdom older than Lilith, younger than the day's dawn, now nestled against him, put up a small thin hand reminiscent of Elena's, and smoothed his cheek.

"I wish you were my daddy, Mr. Potter."

He took the hand and patted it. "You have your own daddy."

The child sighed. "He's such a rotter."

"What!"

"Mommy says so. He doesn't want me to express my talent."

Ancient eyes in a baby face, translucent as green glass, looked up at him.

"I can't blame him. If you were my child, I'd get you out of here quick."

"What would you do with me?"

"Keep you home, send you to school every day, let you play with other children."

"But I love it here."

"I wouldn't let you stay, however much you love it."

She looked sidewise at him and laughed a peal of pretty laughter and slipped away from him.

On the stage Dane was experimenting with the first love scene. Elena paused in the embrace to inquire:

"Tootles, dc I make quick love or slow?"

"How do you feel it?"

She frowned. Her face without makeup was haggard and plain in the merciless overhead light. But this meant nothing. A mood, a flash of laughter, a sudden tear, could change the face into beauty. She was thinking.

"Like this," she said.

Henry Potter watched and was aware of a strange congealing of the blood. She drew away from Bert and approached again, warily, testing him, not for love's sake, for there was no love here, but testing him to see whether he had the magic she needed to rouse her own clamor. Bert in the play was young, a poet as well as a scientist, withdrawn, at once aware and shy, sensitive and passionate, unawakened and quivering. The playwright had portrayed him in living character and the woman, who was now Elena, was older and more experienced, reluctant with disappointment, eager to love again. But she had been too often used without love and unable to love, she longed to be used with love by this pure young man. Ah, but only for her own sake—

He saw the raw sex of what she was doing and could not draw his eyes away. Her fingers now upon the man's neck, smoothing his cheeks, touching the shoulders, fingers following the nerves of his muscles, of his body, to the very soles of his feet, as though she wove an invisible web about him, within which he lay helpless. And Dane presided over this sex play with the closest attention, standing not three feet away, supervising, suggesting, commanding.

"Fingers—fingers—along the inside of the arm—where the skin is most sensitive, at the waist, now—and the inside of the thighs—both hands together in rhythm—"

Bert bit his lips and suddenly leaped to his feet and strode across the stage into the wings. Dane watched without speaking and then called.

"Elena—come here—"

He drew her aside into one of his long whispered communications. The cast waited like statues, this one crouched, that one leaning against a wall, these lying on the floor. The four poker players sat down at a table and picked up their cards, a blond actress and three actors.

At the back of the stage Elena sat with her legs drawn up and her forehead on her knees, listening while Dane whispered. He sat beside her, legs outstretched, one arm about her shoulders. Now and then he pushed back the dank hair from her ear. She did not move.

A strange tensity crept over the stage. What was he saying to her? What action was he describing, what demand did he make upon her now?

She was motionless, she made no response, and suddenly he clapped his hands and leaped to his feet.

"All right, children—we'll take that over again! Where's Bert?"

Nobody knew.

"Go and fetch him, somebody!"

They waited again. Elena did not move. Fifteen minutes. Bert came in, his face waxen, his head hanging.

"In place, children!" Dane smiled. "Mary Jane and Sammy, you are watching what Bert and Elena are doing. You've heard about these goings-on but you've never seen it. Now then, peepers!"

Bert lay down, outstretched upon imagined grass, under an imagined tree. Elena rose slowly to her feet and catlike she came to him, her feet bare. She stood over him, he looked up at her.

"All right," Dane said impatiently. "Use it—use everything you've got. This time don't let him get away."

Elena glanced. "Shall I—"

"Use it—use it—try anything."

She lay down beside Bert, cautiously, silently. She leaned over him and began the long stroking of her fingers. He closed his eyes and set his teeth.

In the shadows of the empty theater, Henry Potter got to his feet and stumbled out into the sunshine. God, he could stand no more of that! Rotten—rotten—and all in the name of art, was it? Exploitation, that's what it was—exploitation of the darkest depths of ancestral man, exploitation of an actor in order to exploit the audience, reducing human creatures to their most helpless element, the animal base which none can escape. He stood staring into the busy street, aware to his own shame of a physical turmoil intolerable at his age and his maturity. How Dane would laugh, if he knew! *But that's art, Henry!*

"Are you all right, sir?"

Beaman was at his elbow, solicitous.

"No, I'm not all right. I feel sick."

"I'd better take you home, sir."

"You'd better."

"Yes, sir."

He spent the rest of the afternoon at home, writing slowly and between intervals a long letter to Ethel, in which he said nothing. The house was silent and peaceful. At four o'clock Nora brought him tea and small sandwiches on a tray and with it letters from Ethel. He ate and drank while he read. One was written in Rio de Janeiro, where Ethel had decided to leave the cruise to stay at a hotel for a while and rejoin the boat when it stopped in Rio on its return leg of the cruise.

"Such peace," she wrote, "and the sea as warm as a bath. Not invigorating, but I don't want to be invigorated. I floated for hours this morning, almost slept in the water. No letter from you, Henry—nothing but a page from Marie, telling me that you are well but they don't see much of you. Have fun, dear—whatever you are doing."

He finished the letter and read the others. She wrote a good letter. And he finished his own letter, assuring her that he was not doing what she thought he was, and when she came back he would tell her all about it, if he could! An hour later, when he was examining his stamp collection, Beaman announced Aubrey Dane, and there he stood on the threshold.

"Bad news, Henry," Dane said. He came in and sat down in a green leather chair. "We have to find a new leading man. Bert doesn't want to go on with the show."

"After today?"

"After today. . . . That's the trouble with these semi-professional amateur types. They get to feeling personal and they quit."

"I thought Bert Jameson had played at least three successful plays in London."

"Still an amateur. He's not been through the grind of methodical training."

Henry Potter attached an old Greek stamp to a page where it belonged. "Maybe he doesn't like the play."

"Of course he likes the play. He doesn't want to act with Elena."

He peered through his small microscope at a new stamp from the People's Republic of China. The paper was poor but the design was rather good.

He put aside the microscope. "Will you answer a question honestly?"

"Why not?" Dane asked. He sauntered to the table where the stamps were lying. "How you can busy yourself over scraps of colored paper!"

"Plenty of history in stamps," he said. "Look at this page—the history of the Chinese empire. Dragon to red star!"

"So what is your question?"

Henry Potter stared down again through his microscope. A new Korean stamp, South Korea. He had not been able to get the set of North Korean stamps he wanted. Without looking up he put his question like an arrow flung from a bow.

"Do you get erotic pleasure from directing a scene such as the one I saw this afternoon?"

A long pause, and still he did not look up.

"No," Dane said at last. "And it is indecent of you to suggest such a thing."

"I'm asking in curiosity." He moistened the edge of a strip of paper with glue.

"Then you have a dirty mind."

"Curiosity simply means that I want information. For if you do find erotic pleasure in creating such scenes out of your imagination, then there is significance to it."

"Suppose I said yes, I do find erotic pleasure? Which I don't, mind you, and I still say you have a dirty mind—"

"Supposing that you do, then a good deal is explained to me of theater nowadays. It's a sort of voyeurism and you're seeking out other voyeurs. You told me you are married?"

"Yes."

"Your wife takes no interest in your activities?"

"My wife understands me. And she doesn't have a dirty mind."

"She never comes to the theater?"

"Oh, yes, she's there. But she's—unobtrusive."

Dane was walking around the handsome room, looking at the book shelves, reading the titles or pretending to, and now he walked to the wide window opening upon a narrow garden two floors below. There he halted, his back to Henry Potter, a slim, graceful figure, elegant, the shoulders unexpectedly broad, the head round, the neck slender but strong. If Ethel were here, she would look at this fellow thoughtfully for a while and then when he was gone, she would tell him exactly what Dane was. Without her, he was not able to diagnose.

Dane turned. "Henry, will you listen to a lecture from me?"

"If it's interesting—"

"It's educational, let's say." Dane sat down in the green chair again and crossed his knees. "Let me begin by affirming that I am not a conceited man."

"Tea?" he inquired.

"No tea, thank you, Henry, and don't interrupt. I am now beginning to think of complex matters and I must put them into terms which a business magnate can understand. I have no money, Henry, and I'm not interested in money unless I can earn it by doing what I enjoy. Would you understand me better if I said that I am like a teacher? Or a preacher? Or a middleman, an entrepreneur of the art of the theater?"

"No, I don't think I'd understand any better," Henry Potter said mildly, "but maybe it is only because I want you to explain yourself. Remember, all I know about the theater is when I go to see a play and I'd rather not hate it. All these preliminary doings I know nothing about."

"It's a business and it's an art," Dane said. "And these actors are my material. No, not even they—it's what they have in them, the talent—I disdain the word, threadbare as it is, but I don't know what else to call it. It's the knack, the wandering gene, the gift an actor carries within himself. It's an itch, an urge to create, but he has no words as a writer has, no ear for music, as a composer has. He has only his body, and so his body is his tool, his means for expressing what is in him, his emotions, his energy. And he can't even use his tool. He's awkward and wordless and doesn't know what to do until the playwright gives him words. Then he doesn't know how to speak them, because he doesn't know how to use his body. That's where I come in. I

tell him how to use his voice, how t
to direct his energy. I can't make
is. I can only make him feel free, I
discover himself. And he can't disco
finds there, and he will never be a g
ever I help him, than the one he di
Sometimes he's intelligent as well as
I'm beside myself with joy. Sometim
his talent is thin and shallow and t
ruthless and tell him that the part is
and he goes away heartbroken, and
I let myself. But I can't afford to let
find someone quickly to take his plac
wait. It's a dichotomy. Actors are sens
yet they must develop hides thick eno
most cruel judgment of all—'you aren't
this part.' "

"Can't you tell him what to do? Isn'
to do it?"

"No. If something goes wrong he has
fall back upon. His source must be in hi
know so well what he has to express t
press it, whatever happens. I don't pl
my actor. I lead—I lead—and only as
go. I open a door as far as he can bea
I never do today what should be done t
if all this makes no sense to you, Henry, t

"It makes a queer sort of sense, in a beg
way. But I still don't see what it has to
making Elena finger a young man's body, e
'Fingers—fingers'—you kept saying. Are
put that scene before the public the way y
this morning?"

"Probably not, but perhaps I shall or will—
two words, I never know which one to use

lore her own powers of rousing a young man. Is
r natural way of doing it? Has she some other way
know nothing about or perhaps that even she
nothing about? I provide a ready-made tech-
and if it works then it's good and if it doesn't
t's no good, and that's about it. When the ready-
doesn't work, still it gives her an idea of what
t, and then she does it herself, and it may be
fully right. I don't go a moment faster than she
ollow out of her own knowledge and imagination.
r instruct before the pupil is ready—that's the first
n in teaching. Don't try to save a soul before it
s to be saved. That's the second axiom in preach-
Never give directions to your cast too soon—that's
e."

ow do you know what you want?"

h, that's *my* talent! I always know what I want.
I know, always, whether an actor can give it to
And when I know he can, gently I persuade him
dozen different ways—dozen? a hundred—that
n trust me because I know he can do it, and there-
he trusts himself. Perfect love casteth out fear. I
out his fear, because I love the thing he can do,
when he feels my love, he loves me in return."

I wish you wouldn't use the word 'love,'" Henry
. He put away his microscope, closed the stamp
k, and took the other green leather chair.

Why not?"

It upsets me, except when it's used in the usual
se."

It is a love process, nevertheless," Dane said. "You
't force a woman against her will, if you want to
ssess her. She must want to be possessed. The actor,
n or woman—"

"Don't confuse the two, I beg you," Henry said.

"Only to the extent of saying that I don't care which it is," Dane said, laughing. "The process is the same. It's first to win confidence in me, and then to transfer that to self-confidence in him—or her."

"You sound like a psychiatrist fellow," Henry said.

"Smile when you say that, Henry," Dane retorted.

"Or a hypnotist," Henry said.

Dane rose. "It's time for me to leave. You're getting funny."

He saluted sharply, wheeled, and left the room. The next instant he was back again at the door, his bright face pale against the shadows. He spoke in a low, still voice, between set teeth.

"That was the goddamndest question! Of course I feel erotic pleasure! How did you know?"

This time he was gone.

Late in the evening Henry finished with his stamps and then locked them into the wall safe behind the picture of his grandfather. The thing was cleverly designed, his own doing, and he was proud of it. The portrait slid silently to the left and revealed the door of the safe. In it he had half a million dollars' worth of rare stamps, and Ethel had her jewels. He peered into the deep vault and saw a familiar small box of crimson velvet. He reached for it, opened it, and saw the necklace of sapphires that he had given her for a wedding present. Wherever they had traveled she had always taken it with her, but this time she had left it behind. He put it back, locked the vault, and slid the picture into place. Two o'clock—it was time he went to bed.

4

When he woke up in the night it was to see an image emerging from the shadows of his brain. No, it had nothing to do with his brain. She was there, Elena appearing from some deeper center in every physical detail. Thus her face, and he had not known until now that her eyes were not dark, as he had supposed, but a very clear green appearing dark merely because they were set in thick black lashes, and her hair which was dark, he now remembered, though tinted with gold, was curled delicately about her ears, and those ears were small and very white. Her skin was white, without color, and her lips were not red. He knew now that he hated lipstick, although he had taken it for granted that all women wore it. How many times when he had been moved to kiss Ethel, if only by way of compliment when she looked handsome in a new outfit, how many times had she not warned him off: "Be careful now, Henry —I have on my war paint!" Yesterday when he sat in the theater, in the front row of seats, he had seen Elena fling herself again and again into embrace, under Dane's direction, and he had wondered instinctively, he now remembered, whether her kiss left a stain. Thinking of such kisses he had felt half ashamed of himself. To Elena these kisses were nothing, a technique of her strange craft. He turned his thoughts sternly to the abstract. When a woman kissed a man as part of the day's work, upon a stage, again and again, practicing to

128

achieve, in appearance at least, the exact amount of passion required to stimulate the imagination of the hundreds of men and women watching in the shadows beyond the footlights, did a kiss elsewhere ever mean anything to her? He pondered the abstract now and in wakefulness, while her image retreated into his brain, conceived a thought so daring that he blushed at his own daring, while he clung to it. . . . Why not ask her?

She came strolling down the aisle the next day to find him where he sat. On the stage Dane was working with the secondary actors and she was released.

"Henry," she called softly and he trembled. Involuntarily he turned to see whether Beaman was present. He was not. It was noon and he had gone to lunch.

"Here at your feet," he replied daringly.

She laughed and sank into the seat beside him.

"Those lights on the stage burn out my eyes. I can't even see somebody as substantial as you are."

She squeezed his arm with both hands. "How are you, Henry, darling? You look so sweet and patient sitting here day after day. Sometimes when I'm discouraged I look for you down here, and see a big shape, a Rock of Gibraltar, and I feel better. Have you ever seen the Rock of Gibraltar, Henry?"

"Yes, more than once."

"What were you doing there?"

"Cruising."

"All by yourself?"

"No."

"You don't want to tell me?"

"With my wife—and friends."

"Will you take me someday? I've never been on a cruise."

"If you're a good girl and make this play a hit, you can go by yourself."

"Then I won't go." She loosed his arm suddenly and brushed back her hair with both hands. "It's getting hot. I wonder what it's like outside—spring, maybe! I don't know. I'm half asleep when I hurry here in the morning, and when I get out it's night. I never see the sun— or the rain."

"It's April," he said.

She leaned her head against his shoulder. "I'm half dead. I couldn't sleep last night."

"Why not?"

"I don't know. Maybe somebody was thinking of me and keeping me awake. I'm psychic."

She was of such strange and sensitive stuff that he could almost believe his own thoughts had wakened her.

"Let me sleep here against your shoulder."

"I'll sit still."

She was silent for a moment and then murmured, "I can feel your warmness right through your sleeve."

He found himself putting his hand on her head, smoothing the soft hair. Her eyes were closed. He drew his hand away.

"Elena—"

"Yes, Henry?"

"Nothing."

It was impossible to ask so foolish a question.

She shook him gently, her hands encircling his arm again, and he was surprised at the sudden strength of those small hands.

"Henry! Tell me—"

"I can't."

"Why not?"

"It's silly, and it's been a long time since I was silly."

She laughed a small clear ripple. "Henry, you're sweet when you're silly. What were you going to say?"

He blurted it out then. "How can you kiss a fellow —a stranger—over and over again—up there—and not have it mean anything—when you might want it to mean everything?"

He stared straight ahead, blushing all over, and waited. He turned his head slightly, glanced at her side-wise and met her eyes gazing up into his. He could have sworn they were black, and knew they were not.

When she spoke it was with an ancient wisdom. "Henry, a kiss doesn't matter unless it's with the body. I don't kiss with the body—only with the mind. It's a job. I study the kiss the way I study my lines. . . . I think . . . when you really kiss you don't think."

"Don't I?"

She gave him an astonished look, a little laugh, and a touch on the cheek with the palm of her hand. "Oh, Henry, you're sweet. Do you mean you don't know?"

She dismissed the conversation and yawned. "I have to go to the bathroom. Tootles is looking around. I must get back on the job."

In a few moments she sauntered up the aisle, climbed upon the stage, and took her position. Bert, having persuaded himself to stay with the show, waited ex-pectantly. Two minutes later she was practicing the kiss. She had told the truth. The kiss, so carefully prac-ticed and now perfectly performed, was entirely unreal.

The episode of the kiss, as he called it secretly now, began to develop into what he frankly, although always secretly, recognized as an obsession. Upon the walls of the small picture gallery on the third floor of his house there hung three paintings by Salvador Dali. Ethel had bought them in the Dali period of her life, which he connected with the approach of middle age, and had consequently intensely disliked, until one day he had paused on a street in lower New York to look at some sidewalk pictures, exhibited by a young man with a black patch over his right eye. One of the pictures had so astonished him that he was moved to inquire what it meant. It was the painting of a huge left eye, protruding from a stem like the horn of a snail. The right eye was lost in the small obscure face, and around the face, but especially around the big protruding eye, the body trunk, the arms, the legs, curled in deformed dependent weakness.

"All you have to do is look at me," the young man had said brusquely. "I'm totally dependent on my one good eye. What it sees is all I see of life. It tells me what food is good, where the street is, and where the girl's mouth is. Sometimes it misleads me, and I'm way off. But it's all I've got."

The eye had become the obsession.

Remembering this young man tonight, he climbed the stairs before starting to bed and stood before the Dali paintings. He could paint a thing himself. It would be a girl's mouth, the lips full but delicately cut. That was all. Just her mouth. Face and body belonged to it, of course, but he could only see the mouth, dream of the lips, dwell upon them, possessed. He laughed silently and grimly. Old fool! What Ethel would say if she knew! He was amazed and yet not in the least ashamed of himself, he discovered to his further amazement. His own lips suddenly burned. He had no idea there was so much youth left in him, or was it possible that youth never died in man or woman? Ethel's father, for example, who lay invalid for many years before he died, his brain attacked by clots of dead blood, had still been young in some instinct unconnected with the brain. He remembered that the nurse, scolding and laughing, had stayed out of his reach.

"Naughty-naughty! I have to wash you, old boy! Just keep your hands to yourself. . . . Did you ever? The devil never dies, they say!"

He turned away from the Dali paintings, revolted by this memory of his father-in-law and the buxom nurse. Ethel's mother, he remembered, had been saddened by the story, but in her remote and dignified way she had forgiven her husband, suppressing, he now imagined, her own memories which she could not quite forgive.

And yet he was not revolted now by himself. Instead he felt a tenderness, sweet and restorative, when he thought of Elena. That her lips were the focal point, Daliesque, simply meant—what? He went downstairs and lay down for a while upon the couch in the library, curiously relaxed as though he had yielded himself at last in some struggle he had not acknowledged. Whatever was to happen would happen. A youthful warmth invaded his body, not to be called love, a fondness, perhaps an interest, innocent until proved otherwise. He rose, restless, and decided to return to the theater. Dane was rehearsing now night and day.

He chose a seat far back, so that no one knew he was there. The theater was dark except for the lights above the stage, and at this distance he could not hear Dane's voice, directing in low tones. The silence was absolute as the actors took their places for the first scene of the first act. Elena entered. She was Jennet, a woman busy about her daily tasks in a house in the desert, a shack of a house, which she was trying to make into a home, a froth of curtain stuff hung over her arm. He had never seen the play entire, and he had not been able to piece together the fragments. He had read it many times, and he knew the story as he knew the story of his own life, but reading and knowing were very different from what he now saw. How direct the transmission from eye to brain! A picture is better than a thousand words, some old Chinese sage had once said, and there he saw the picture. Elena? No, a woman, not Elena. Instead of that small, restless, disorganized human creature he saw a composed and beautiful woman, young, happy, busy, a woman who might have been any woman, her hair brushed back from her face, her blue cotton frock fresh for the morning. She was building her nest as a bird builds a nest. A child ran in, with a playmate, the sort of thing that could happen in a million houses at nine o'clock of a Saturday morning. The neighbor boy wanted to swim in the pool. Yes, the warm young mother said, why not? They would all swim, a fine day for it, the sun hot, and the curtains could wait. . . . And was this Elena? This laughing young mother, as simple as dawn, fed upon simple food, simple and content? He was not in the least attracted to her. She was the ubiquitous American woman, a good wife, a good mother, the lover already lost in marriage. But how did Elena know?

Dane was speaking to her, she stopped to listen, and for a moment Elena was there. Only for a moment. She repeated a gesture, and the play went on. The children ran out and she, about to follow, paused at the door. A man entered, Jerome—a scientist, older than she, her husband, the lover lost in science. A conversation of commonplace, a guest expected, a young man from England. Someone they had known together years ago—ah, they had once been in England? Yes, they had met there, she and the husband, somehow. He knew how, but Elena was making it all fresh, as though he had no memory of what he had read. No, this was not an ordinary house. It was a house in the desert, and not their home. She had come with her husband here to the desert, a following wife, he entangled in his work, a creation of some sort, a critical possibility for life or death. Not a weapon, he assured her, but an advance, in this day of advance, which would put the nation far ahead of every possible enemy. But he had struck an impasse. He needed another brain, and so he had sent for the one he valued most. It was lodged in the skull of the guest, the Englishman, young and a genius.

"Children!" Dane called. "Take your five minutes. Hell, I'll make it ten. You're doing nicely, my little ones!"

The play broke abruptly and she was Elena again. She rubbed her hands over her face, tangled her hair, and walked across the stage and leaned against Dane. He put an arm about her waist, kissed her cheek, pushed her off, and began a murmured conversation with the stage manager.

"I have to go to the bathroom!" Elena announced.

Nobody answered, the cast had already dispersed themselves. She walked down the aisle into the lobby and did not come back. Ten minutes passed. The assistant director shouted, "Cast! Second scene!"

They hurried in from the wings and waited. Elena did not come. Dane tapped the back of a chair with his ruler.

"Where is Elena?"

At this moment she appeared, running like a child, and stopped. "Henry, I didn't know you were here!"

"I've been watching you."

"Have you? I thought I felt my old Rock of Gibraltar somewhere!"

Dane was staring into the darkness.

"Elena!"

"Coming! Henry, wait for me afterwards?"

"Yes."

She danced down the aisle to the stage and he sat in a state of bemusement waiting for the night to begin.

At two o'clock in the morning the streets of New York are quiet and beautiful. He knew them well, for when he was young he had walked them alone, restless with hurt and anger, driven from his house by his wife, the young Ethel, who maintained those private rights never mentioned by the church in their wedding ceremony. He had not thought of these rights, until one day in Poona, India, years later. They had attended the wedding of an Indian friend, Sri Jagdesh Singh. There, as the Indian couple sat by the sacred fire burning upon a small central hearth, they on one side and the holy man on the other, he and Ethel had heard certain words pronounced by the bride's father. The requirements were familiar, children to be welcomed, property to be shared. Then came the difference. The father of that slim dark little bride, an immensely fat man made more huge by his knee-length coat of silver and blue brocade, put his final solemn command to the tall handsome young man who now possessed his daughter. The father spoke in deep solemnity.

"You shall not force her against her will, for her right is over her own person."

At his side Ethel had suddenly sighed. "How civilized! How comforting to the bride on the eve of her wedding night!"

They had exchanged a deep look, he and Ethel, and she was suddenly defiant. "Well, I mean it!"

They had turned away from each other then, neither of them able to bear the memory of a struggle begun on their wedding night and continued through at least five years. It was the war of possession. Was her body his or hers? How stupid he had been not to realize at once that what was taken by force or by right was never given and therefore could not be possessed! When at last he had been compelled to understand that she could not give herself against her will, they had come close to parting, except that they had continued to love one another, and any suffering more acute than this war between lovers was not within his experience. The hours that he had walked these streets! The times he had refused the empty consolations of women, accosting him! He had wished in those lonely hours that he could have been consoled by a woman, any woman, and he might have been, had he not been desperately in love with Ethel, lying straight and still in her bed, obdurate, unyielding and, he thought, cold. One night he had broken completely, his will gone, and longing only to be near her on any terms rather than cast into his outer darkness of cosmic loneliness, he had rushed back to the house to throw himself on his knees beside her bed.

"I'll never come near you again," he had cried. "I'll move into another room. I'll never touch you. . . . But I can't live away from you."

He had pressed his face into her pillow, had breathed in the faint scent of her, had waited, humbled and shattered, expecting nothing. And then out of the silence she stirred, she moved toward him, and he heard her sob. 'But I—I want you to love me! I want you—I want you—"

He had made a great cry and together they achieved a height of love which he had never imagined. She was passionate. He discovered this after five years of marriage.

Waiting outside the theater for Elena, his mind returned to those unhappy years. He was not unhappy now, nor had he ceased to love Ethel. Why then did he feel this renewed disturbance? He had no wish to pursue Elena and no need to do so. Eroticism for its own sake had never interested or even amused him. Why be entangled in the weeds of love when he had his own garden? He had watched sundry friends of his embroil themselves in affairs which could have no end except that of trouble and embarrassment, and above all, for him, the loss of dignity. He had not enjoyed bathroom humor since his eighth year, and before he was twenty mere sexual prowess appeared only as adolescence in parade, the conversation of garage hands and truck drivers. With Ethel, after that night which was his true marriage night, there had been no inhibitions. It became exciting to watch her at a dinner party, or in their box at the opera, remote and handsome, and remember in deep male pride, this same woman abandoned to him by her own will. No courtesan or concubine could have provided such excitement—a queen, perhaps, an empress, but no lesser one. He had his secret knowledge, his private delight. Their mutual satisfaction was their mutual guarantee against invaders.

And now here was Elena, tripping out of the shadows of the stage door, conveniently ahead of the others so that he need not be seen with her. She locked her hands over his arm.

"Let's run! Run, run before the tyrant cries halt!"

They ran and turned down an empty side street and she pulled him into a doorway, laughing silently. She made a great sigh and threw herself into his arms.

"Oh, Henry, you're sweet! I was so afraid Tootles would get me!"

She kissed one cheek and the other and then kissed him full on the lips. Physical response, automatic and

instinctive, infused his blood. He closed his arms about
her and when she turned her head, he lifted his right
hand and held her head and pressed her mouth against
his and as suddenly released her, to stand trembling.

"Why, Henry," she said softly. "I didn't know you
could! Shall we do it again?"

"No," he said shortly.

They walked in silence, she clinging to his arm in
her favorite pose, hands clasped together. After a
while she began to sing to the moon, very softly, and
there the moon hung, enormous over the towers. He
had never walked the empty streets of night in this
mood before and his heart dissolved in a happiness
entirely physical, a tenderness too deep for passion, a
sensation that took him back to adolescence. This was
the sort of thing he had felt when he first began to
dream of girls. Elena made him young again. She was
a girl, and he was a boy. Yet had she offered herself to
him he would have drawn back, repelled.

"You should be asleep," he said gently.

"I can't sleep," she said. "I'm too happy."

She waited for him to ask her the source of her happiness, and he could not. He did not want to talk or to
hear her talk. He wanted only feeling, her hands clasped
on his arm, the warmth of her thigh pressed against his
as they walked in step. Only at last when they were
near her hotel did he draw her into a doorway. For now
he was overcome with desire to feel her lips again upon
his, and he kissed her again but gently. Then he lifted
his hands and drew her head back to see her face in the
moonlight. What was the terrifying magic in this face,
the curve of the lips, the line of the hair dark against
her brow, the shape of the eyes, a physical magic in
every curve and line? He did not know what she was, or
care. Good or evil, wise or foolish, clever, stupid, a

child, a woman, let her be ever so weak and willful and all that he could not admire, this body held the power over him. No, not over him but over an unknown depth in his being. Somewhere in his ancestry had there once lived a man who had loved a woman with this face, this body? But he did not love Elena.

"Will you come in, Henry?" she whispered.

His hands dropped. "No," he said. "I will not. . . . Goodnight, Elena."

He walked away and left her there. When he looked back, she was gone.

The trees were in leaf along the street and spring was established. Carts of flowers stood at the street corners and in the windows of florist shops, daffodils and hyacinths and tulips spread the news of the season. He got out of his car at the door of the tall building which he owned and told the doorman to send the gardener to him at twelve o'clock. The evergreens at the entrance must be changed for willows.

He was early as usual, and this morning earlier than ever because of last night, escape, no doubt, but here he was, seeking immersion again in the still waters of his business, the green pastures of his everyday world. He sat down behind his desk. Marie had put yesterday's mail ready for him and he glanced through the pages. The Chamber of Commerce of New York wanted a speech on foreign trade. The Overseas Press Club wanted an address on trade with mainland China. The Rotary annual meeting wanted a talk on the social responsibilities of the industrialist in a free society. A minor shareowner wanted to know about dividends, a political analyst in Washington wanted to know whether his firm could supply cleaning equipment to a hotel in New Delhi, India. The dean of the summer school of a western university wanted to know if he could include a tour for teachers through one of the Potter factories. A dealer in Duluth reported a fair trade violation. A dealer in Austin, Texas, inquired about cooperative advertising. A distributor from Japan was to arrive a week from Thursday. A meeting of the budget board, a luncheon for a visiting industrialist from West Germany, an article for the company newspaper on the new pension plan, discuss with the third vice-president a new appointment to the sales department . . . he pressed a button.

Marie came in looking more than ever like dried seaweed. He dictated for two hours, his mind absorbed, concentrated, yet aware of the stir beneath. Twelve o'clock! The cast was gathering on the stage. Elena would be dancing about on one foot and the other, limbering, she called it. He would not see her today. Let him live with this stir in the blood, observe its effect, analyze, if he could, what it meant, decide, if he could, how to cast it out of his being. He ordered luncheon brought to his desk at half past one and dismissed the subdued but sullen Marie. At half past two the telephone rang. He took up the receiver and heard Elena sobbing.

"Oh, Henry, darling, I—I need you—terribly! Please come!" He prayed that Marie was not listening. "What's the matter?"

"I can't go on with the show—I can't—I can't."

"Why not?"

"Tootles simply can't direct! He doesn't understand me! He's ruining everything!"

"Elena, listen to me. Stop crying. Sit down somewhere quietly and wait. I'm coming."

He reached for his hat and coat and left. To fortify his own resolution this morning, he had told Beaman not to return until five o'clock. He caught a taxi and fifteen minutes later strode into a storm. The assistant director was on the stage working with the minor actors. Aubrey Dane was not there, and he discovered Elena, after peering through the darkness, in the most distant seat of the empty theater. Her head was thrown back, her hair flowing from her forehead. Her eyes were closed. He put his hand gently on her shoulder. She gave a start.

"Oh, Henry—"

"I came as quickly as I could."

"Where can we talk? In the back row—"

She clutched his hand, her fingers entwined in his, and he felt no withdrawal in himself, her flesh like his own, a marvel to him, who had only distaste until now. Had she been his daughter he might have felt this sameness, but she was not his daughter. They slipped into seats in a darkened corner, her hand still in his.

"Henry, try to understand me!"

"Yes, Elena."

"I've found out what's the matter—why I can't perform. I've had such queer stifled feelings. Nothing flows out of me. I know my lines, but simply nothing happens. It's the director—I hate him, Henry. I want him changed. I have to have someone who sympathizes with me. He leaves me cold because he's cold. And I'm an artist, Henry. I can't work with someone who's cold. Henry, I must have another director."

"He doesn't act cold."

She gave a wail of distress. "Henry, don't defend him! I can't bear it. You're the only friend I have, Henry. Everybody hates me—yes, they do!"

For he was shaking his head. Then he saw that she was trembling, and tears were gathering in her immense dark eyes. They rolled down her cheeks in round drops and he watched, fascinated. She was irresistible. He found her other hand and held both in his, cold small hands, quivering.

"There now—don't cry, Elena. Nothing's so bad that it can't be mended."

She sobbed softly and slipped into his arms, her head against his breast.

"There now," he muttered. "There now—I'll speak to him, honey—I'll speak to him—"

She lifted her head suddenly and sharply. "Speaking won't do any good. You don't know him. He'll not listen to you. I want you to get him out, Henry. I want you to get him out of the theater and out of the play— out—out—out! I don't want to see him anywhere around—ever!"

"But it's his play, Elena—he's the producer, too."

"You've put in the money, haven't you? Then fire him—"

"But a play has to have a director."

"Not this one—there are plenty of good ones—others —better than he is."

"He's had successes and—"

"Not this kind of a play, Henry—"

Aubrey Dane came out of the wings and stared down into the shadows.

"Elena!"

His voice commanded and instinctively she rose to obey, then paused.

"Henry—I swear to you—I'll not rehearse again. This is the last time—unless you get him out." She ran down the aisle as swiftly as a child runs, sprang upon the stage, and took her position.

Alone in the shadows he watched, amazed and confused. In half-conscious assessment of her unreason, he felt in his entrails her every movement, her grace, the shape and turn of her head, the sound of her voice, a physical enchantment having nothing to do with what she was. He got up, alarmed anew, fumbled for his hat, and went away to walk the streets and face the fact that he had fallen into some sort of love that he did not like and yet could not resist.

Then should he not send for Ethel? In the clear air of her commonsense this miasmic obsession would fade and he could resume his own being again. Seeing nothing of the people hurrying past him, to and fro, and all but killed when he crossed a street against the light, he discovered the frightful fact that he did not want Ethel to come home and that he did want to pursue this new emotion centered in some unexplored region of his being. He went into a bar and lingered over a Scotch. He bought a pack of cigarettes and smoked a chain of them. He had not smoked for years and here he was, at it again, though it had taken him two years to break off under his doctor's orders. He decided that he would not send for Ethel but that he would be prudent. He would not allow Elena to fasten on him or make demands beyond the production of the play. He would allow himself to be amused, even absorbed, temporarily, but he would not allow the stir below his midriff to proceed beyond the command of his cool brain. He would remain in control.

Upon this decision he went back not to the theater but to his office. Marie came in and looked at him shrewishly. "There's a woman been calling you every fifteen minutes. Name's Elena."

He met her small, suspicious eyes. "Tell her I'm not in. And telegraph the west coast plant that I'll be there to inspect the plant tomorrow."

"You can't," she said flatly. "Not if you want to testify at the hearings for that new bill that is coming up in Congress. You'd have to be in Washington tomorrow."

"Very well," he said. "Washington tomorrow and the west coast the next day."

"You want to be at the staff meeting this afternoon?"

"Of course," he said smoothly. "Tell Stanton I'll preside."

He took his accustomed seat in the board room conscious that he had missed three meetings. One meeting he often missed, on the theory that his executives should learn how to conduct the business without him, but he had not missed more than one in succession since his trip to India last year. He was well aware of the surprise pleasantly hidden as each man entered the room and took his place, but he greeted them as though he had been with them each week, and when they were seated he opened the meeting. He had learned long ago how to manage them, how to get them to talk and how to get them to stop talking. He glanced over reports and memoranda, skipping the pages until the summary on the final page. Now, as usual, he waited until quiet pervaded the room, until their eyes were upon him, and then he began.

"I have read your reports, excellent on the whole, but it is obvious to me, as I am sure it is to you, that we have not yet solved in the laboratories the primary problem of the metal that we need for the new machines, powered by high-voltage centers. Two possibilities have been presented to me, the first one based on aluminum, the second on a basalt derivative. In your opinion, gentlemen, and I take it that you have been in close touch with the laboratories both here and on the west coast, which of these two should we use first—experimentally, of course?"

He waited in self-imposed silence, which experience had taught him could last for a full minute. Before the minute was up his quick-thinking men would have begun to talk. Silence troubled them, and they had ideas. He would let them talk while he listened, but at some point he would have to stop the talk, or they would begin to vie with one another to see who could hold his attention. Meanwhile the slow thinkers, the ones he depended upon eventually as checks and brakes upon the talkers and quick ones, would gather their thoughts, ponder the question, make up their minds. If they had not made up their minds he would seize the pause between the quicks and the slows and issue the command he had already decided upon before he came to the meeting.

It arrived, a silence he allowed for ten seconds. None of the slow spoke and before a quick one began again, he spoke.

"What all of you say interests me very much. I take it that we are agreed. The aluminum alloy is the more promising. We will proceed with it here, where we can watch it day by day, but we will assign the basalt experiment to the west coast for further details of development. It may be that we shall use both, unless some serious fault shows up. Thank you, gentlemen! Now let us proceed to methods."

The meeting lasted exactly an hour and a half, the time allowed on his private schedule. Had it run beyond, Marie would have appeared at the door and announced a long-distance call from Washington, which she had previously arranged. He dismissed them and returned to his desk, conscious that his brain had been working with faithful concentration, in spite of the commotion in his vitals and in his blood. He had not for one moment forgotten Elena, but he would not call her. He was in control.

When he entered his office he found Aubrey Dane sitting there, half asleep, his hands in his pockets. He woke, smiled, and got up.

"Sit down, Dane," he said, and seated himself behind the desk. "What are you doing here?"

"I'm here to protest," Dane replied. He sat down again.

"Protest?"

"Our wonder girl," Dane said, "our tinsel star, tells me that you want to fire me."

"Nonsense," he said. "I can't fire you any more than you can fire me. What's the fight between you two?"

"She's scared," Dane said. "She wants to blame everybody except herself. The sad truth is she's not building into the part. Play's too big for her. She can't do it. Maybe we do have to fire her, Henry."

He felt a wrench in his middle. "It's too late for that. Besides, I thought you were crazy about her."

"I'm not crazy about anybody," Dane said. "Certainly not about any actress."

"You act crazy when you're with her!"

"To fatten up her skinny little ego, I tell you! She's got to believe she's great and maybe she will be half-great. It's my business to find out just how great she can be. I still don't know. I've got to get her over this stage of hating me and wanting to get rid of me before I can find out. If I can't get her over it then I'll have to fire her. I told you—it's my function—my duty if you like, certainly my job—to release somehow her inner self, her capacity, her potential, whatever we call it. I'm beginning to wonder how much there is to release. I've got to know within the next day or so. She's important."

"Important."

"She's key. If she can't be freed from the inside, the others can't. And if they can't the audience can't. That's theater, Henry. If it's successful, if the inner being is released, playwright, actors, audience, then we've got great theater. It all depends on me. I've got to find out how much Elena has inside. And I'm beginning to be afraid."

"Maybe the play's not right for her."

"Ah, I thought you'd say that! It would be easier to let her go, Henry. The play's the thing, remember—an ancient truth. Change the star but not the play. Oh, damn this star business! We ought not to have stars. We ought to have just good actors in good plays. But the audience is spoiled. They want glamor with their plays, not good glamor but this false stuff—forty-two, twenty-four, thirty-eight, and all that goes with it. Opening nights break my heart—know why? Those people sitting out there in the dark waiting to be given bread, but they don't even recognize the taste of bread. So when it's offered to them, they don't want it because it isn't cake, the bakers' kind of cake with synthetic frosting. And I want this play to be bread, Henry, and I want them to take and eat. Don't ask me to change the play to suit Elena. I won't do it. The play's got a premise and the premise is worked out with classical soundness."

They were gazing at each other, intent. He turned away first. "Dane, you might try half a dozen stars, if there are that many, which I doubt, and not get one better."

Dane stared at him. "Henry, I believe it's you who have the itch!"

He blushed and hated himself furiously. "I'm a businessman. I want this play to succeed."

"At all costs?"

"Of course—how else does anything succeed—once you've decided to do it?"

"Even the cost of my withdrawing from the project?" Dane asked.

"You can't," he said bluntly. "I'd sue you to the amount of money I've put into the show."

"You wouldn't."

"I would!"

Aubrey Dane got up and whistled softly. "I wouldn't have believed it."

"You don't know me."

"I see I don't. And I see something else. I see that Elena has done to you what she's done to plenty of other men. She's snaked herself inside you like a lovely serpent."

"I deny it." He laughed and put out his hand. "Come on, Dane, we've begun something together. Let's finish it."

Dane hesitated, then he put out his hand. "All right—all right, we'll finish it. But I want to tell you something. In life you can get away with anything. Rain falls on the just and the unjust, and so forth. But in the theater you can't get away with a thing. The heart of drama is that good wins and evil loses. If you compromise with that old-fashioned truth, you lose in the end. I believe it, Henry, though I live by compromise."

"I don't know what you're talking about, Dane."

"I know you don't. Neither do I, maybe. But if the play is to be changed to suit our glittering little star, it's time for me to introduce the playwright. . . . I need support. Here it is."

He opened the door with a flourish and called softly. A slender young woman came in. She wore a dark green suit and no hat and her black hair was smoothly cut to fit a well-shaped head.

"Mr. Potter, meet my wife. . . ."

He rose. "Come in," he said. "I'm surprised to meet you. And I think it's not quite fair of you, Dane."

The young woman came in, drew off her gloves, and sat down in the red leather chair in the corner of the room. "It is my fault, Mr. Potter," she said. "I wasn't willing for him to tell anyone. It's my first play. I wanted to be a stranger." Her voice was quiet and soft.

"Well!" He sat down and looked at her. A nice-looking young woman, not pretty and not plain, with a handsome pair of clear gray eyes and a good smile. "Why do you want to be a stranger?"

"For no favors," she said. "Not to be somebody's wife. Aubrey has become famous, in a way. I'd like to stay a stranger, if you'll let me. I'd not have come today except that Aubrey asked me to—on account of Elena."

"What have you to say to Elena?"

"I don't know until I see her."

"Shall you introduce yourself as the playwright?"

"No. But I'll find out what she needs. I'll help at a distance, if I can."

Her calm was extraordinary, a profound composure to which he was not accustomed. Ethel was composed, but this was peace.

"Why do you write plays?"

"I suppose," she said thoughtfully, "because theater is a place where I can dream. There's no reality to stop me."

"Where have you been?"

"Everywhere. I've lived in Europe—in England—my father was—"

She bit her lip and looked at Dane.

"Why not?" he asked.

"It doesn't matter who my father was. Or even who I am."

"And this play? Is it sacred? Not to be changed?"

"Oh, no, not sacred at all. If there's a way to write it for Elena, why not? Every play's a sort of bridge of dreams—hers, mine, Aubrey's, even yours, Mr. Potter."

"What's your name?" he asked.

"Stella."

He did not repeat the name. He did not like the easy familiarity of theater people, first names at first glance, and forgotten when the play was over. A name was more than a handle, or should be. She sat there, cool and withdrawn, her eyes very clear. She looked at Dane, and he saw a smile flash between them. They were on good terms, then—how deep?

"You don't mind his shenanigans with a beautiful star, Mrs. Dane?"

"It's a hazard of the business."

She looked at Dane with the same placid gaze, powerful in its calm.

The atmosphere in the theater tightened. Voices were tense and tempers short.

Three weeks to go, and though Elena had not carried out her threat, she had not yielded herself. She was fighting her part, stopping to criticize, stopping to protest, stopping to pout, stopping—stopping—

He turned to the quiet woman beside him. "How do you explain this?"

"Frightened," Stella Dane said. "This part is very different from anything she's done before. She can't make mistakes here. There are no retakes."

"So what do we do?"

"Somebody's got to help her."

"Can't you?"

"Me? I'm a woman. Women don't exist for Elena."

"Can you spare Aubrey?"

She laughed silently behind a narrow, firm, sun-browned hand. "Aubrey? She'd see through him. That's the trouble. She has seen through him! She's an honest streak in her. I like her."

"That's a queer thing for a wife to say."

"I'm a queer wife."

She was talking without moving her eyes from the stage, her soft voice always controlled.

"Isn't Aubrey honest?"

"To a point."

"And the point?"

"He'll go as far as he can to save the play—he'll do a good job of pretending. It's not quite pretending. It's genuine interest in the personality and genuine wish to draw out what's there. But when the woman demands something real from him, something beyond the play, well, that's the point. He won't go beyond artistic interest in her."

"You trust him, then."

"As far as is humanly possible for a woman to trust a man."

"Now what does that mean?" He found himself interested in this quiet, withdrawn woman.

"It means that one day there may be someone who can persuade him beyond the point. After all, he's still young. His will may hold. I think so. But—"

"But what?"

"So many available women in this city!"

"Is he strong?"

"I think so. At least he's classified himself."

"Classified?"

"Yes. Love in one compartment, work in another, and never the twain shall meet. So far! And Elena has found this out. She can't break through and she's angry—she's taking it out on him. I've seen it before."

"Are all actresses like this?"

"I don't know them."

"Perhaps I ought to ask, are all women like this?"

"If they are still searching—yes."

"Searching for what?"

"There's only one search for a woman, the search for a man. Though purposes vary."

"Elena is searching for a man?"

"Yes. She needs a source of creative energy. She doesn't have the source within herself, and so she has to find it in someone else. She can find it only in a man."

She turned her calm face to look at him. "Didn't you know any of this before?"

"I haven't thought of such things. I'm a businessman."

"What are you doing here?"

"We seem to need money here as well as everywhere else."

"Oh—"

She turned away and fell into silence. He saw her scribble a few notes in a small book she took from her handbag and he knew himself forgotten.

On the stage Aubrey Dane threw down his script. "We're getting nowhere. If this goes on we can't possibly open on the twenty-fourth."

Elena tossed back her hair. "That's what I've been saying! I tell you the play's got to be rewritten. I just can't say these lines. Nobody could. Unless the fault's in the direction—"

"The fault is in everybody but you, sweetheart," Dane said in cold fury. "You, darling, are the one who is so perfect that none of us can stand up to you —or stand you, to put it bluntly! You're demoralizing the cast. In all my years I've never—but never, sweetie —met an actress who deliberately destroys herself by destroying everything she needs to be a success—the play, the director, the cast! It's suicide. If you were a man, which God knows you're not, I'd remind you that when Samson pulled down the temple he went down with the ruin."

"Who's Samson?"

"Haven't you seen the movie? I take it for granted you can't read."

"I only make movies. I don't go to them."

"Ah then—you wouldn't know. . . . Break for lunch!"

He strode offstage, and Stella slipped from her seat and disappeared. Henry Potter sat watching while the cast went away, one by one, and Elena was left alone on the stage. She sat, elbows on her knees, her head in her hands, hair hiding her face. She looked up suddenly into the darkness of the theater, and seeing no one, for he was in the shadows, she began to weep softly but aloud. His heart turned to a soft and quivering thing in his breast and he got up and went toward her, emerging from the darkness to appear at the foot of the stage.

"Elena!"

She looked up and the light shone on her tears. "Henry—darling! Where did you come from? I was looking for you. I couldn't see you. Oh, Henry, take me away!"

"You need something to eat. You're tired."

"I'm tired." She came to the edge of the stage and

held out her arms like a child. He lifted her down and she clung to him, frantic and sobbing again.

"Henry, I want to go home. I don't like it here in New York. It's so gray all the time. The sun doesn't shine. And I'm used to the sun. And I'm so lonely in that old hotel. At night I'm so lonely."

"How would you like to go to the seashore for a day or so?"

He actually heard himself say these words. He heard his voice speak, he felt his heart pound, and he was terrified. She lifted her head and he looked down into a glorified face. "Henry! Would you——"

"I have a house there—I'll send the servants down to open it."

"No servants, please, Henry—just you and me!"

His silence stopped her.

"You're not afraid of me, Henry?"

"Too old to be afraid," he said lightly. "So be a good girl, Elena. Don't fight with the director any more. Do what he says for the next two days and then beg off for Saturday and Sunday. Your understudy can take your place—she'll be glad enough and you can lie on the beach in the sun and sleep and sleep and get yourself happy again."

"Oh, Henry, I promise! I'll be good."

He had an afterthought. "Don't tell anybody."

"Oh, I wouldn't. That would spoil everything. Now let's have something to eat. I'm starved."

The waves rolled gently upon the white sand, etching faint lines in the rhythm of the sea. Under a clear blue sky the water, a deeper blue, melted into the horizon. Elena lay outstretched, lovely legs and slender arms outflung to the sun, her eyes closed and wet hair spread in an aureole about her face. He saw all this in a glance and then stared resolutely out to sea.

"What are you thinking about, Henry?"

He did not turn at the sound of her voice. "Business."

"Don't think about business, Henry."

"A businessman always thinks about business—that is, if he's at the top."

"Don't you ever play?"

"My best ideas come to me when I'm doing what you call playing. Walking around a golf course—tennis court in the winter—here, on this very beach, for example, I've solved one of my biggest problems."

"What was it?"

"How to get my inventors to work with my plants in Europe and Asia instead of thinking their ideas over there are no good."

"Who was with you on the beach then, Henry?"

"My wife."

The mention of Ethel was his protection against Elena and against himself. It was hard to think of Ethel, yet she was alive and would return, and he wanted her to return, and even wished that he knew where she was at this moment. He had had no letters this week. And they had never been separated so long before. Was it possible that Marie was sending her misinformation? He had made no secret of his coming to the seashore.

"Marie, I'm taking Elena to the beach house for the weekend. She's worn out and endangering the play."

"What play?" Marie had inquired with affected stupidity.

"I daresay you know all about it," he had growled.

"I don't know anything until and unless you tell me, Mr. Potter," she had said primly.

"Well, I'm taking a flier in the theater," he said carelessly. "Something new for a change, instead of a vacation."

She had said nothing to this, but her small gray eyes blinked behind their spectacles. He felt her agonized devotion and thrust it off as he had so often. "Now don't sit there and look like a tabby cat watching a mouse! Whatever you're thinking, it isn't so. It all began one night when my wife and I went to a play—a rotten piece of goods, if ever I saw one. And I made up my mind I'd do something about it. I suppose a playwright has the freedom to open up his shirt and show his cancer to the public if he wants to. But one cancer looks like another and after I've seen one, I've seen it. I'd like to see something else once in a while—a couple of healthy people for a change."

"People like to see cancers, Mr. Potter," Marie had said.

He had turned on her sharply. "Do you, Marie?"

"I kind of like to see people doing things I wouldn't dare do myself, and don't want to do, Mr. Potter. It's exciting."

This from a tabby cat! He thought of it now as he gazed out to sea. Things that he would not dare to do himself and didn't want to do, but exciting, nevertheless—and at this moment he felt a soft brush of hair on his bare thigh. Elena had moved. Her head lay on his leg. He looked down upon her sun-warmed face, and into her dark eyes. She yawned and he saw the inside of her mouth, pink and clean as a child's, the teeth white and even. Her breath was sweet.

"I'm sleepy," she said.

She closed her eyes and her extravagant lashes rested

upon her cheeks. Images of what he might do, did not dare to do, did not want to do, rose to his mind, organic and separate. They had nothing to do with his usual self, his real self, if he knew himself, which he doubted. And a fragment of wisdom had come from the last person in the world whom he could suspect of wisdom. Marie, his old-maid secretary. Damn her for intruding at this moment, when she was the last person of whom he wished to think, with this child of a woman pillowed upon his thighs. She was so young, this Elena, so young and so beautiful in her sleep. He had not realized how beautiful she really was until now when he could examine her face, the flawless skin, the perfect mouth, full and delicate at the same time, the small straight nose, eyebrows—what was it a Chinese had said about eyebrows? Several words, brushed by a poet centuries ago, "brows of beauty above eyes of loveliness."

He put his hand softly against the crown of her hair and saw with a strange pang how old his hand was, an old man's hand, the veins already beginning to protrude, a bony hand, and his naked legs, those of an aging man, and though he was slim, his flesh was no longer firm and smooth. Against her utter youth he saw himself years older than she, and he was suddenly lonely and lost. He did not want to grow old, and he was not old, his inner being, heart and soul, as young as ever. He was the same person that he had been at twelve and at sixteen and at twenty-five and thirty-five and throughout the years, and with the same yearning for love, the ready passion, the need—

He bent down with an impulsiveness he had forgotten and kissed her softly on the lips.

She opened her eyes. "I've been waiting for that."

He laughed. "You haven't been asleep, you rascal!"

She smiled a soft and lazy smile. "You're awfully hard to get, Henry—you know that?"

"I didn't know you wanted to get me, as you put it."

"I need you, Henry."

He gazed down into those dark and liquid eyes, fascinated and appalled, and he managed to force himself to speak.

"Honey, I'm an old man."

She spoke with a flash of sudden anger. "Don't call me 'honey'! Don't call me any of those silly love names! They're all spoiled, because silly directors think we like to hear them. They think we think they mean love. They don't—and we know it."

This was no child! "Now that's clever of you, Elena. I've wondered if you saw through it."

"I see through him," she said, "and I'm sad. I wish he wouldn't call me sweetheart and darling and all that—crap."

"Why?"

"Because someday—I might fall truly in love—as I hope and dream to do—and then all the beautiful and tender old words for love will be—useless. How shall I tell my love that I—love him? The very word 'love' is used up—dead. What other words are there, Henry?"

She had slipped away from him. Discussing love, he knew that he was saved. "I don't know, Elena."

"But you love your wife?"

"Yes."

"So what words do you say?"

"I don't know what words I'll say now."

She sat up, honestly concerned. "Oh, poor Henry, we've spoiled the words for you, too—with our make-believe love—"

He got to his feet. "Come—I'll race you to that rock."

She ran after him down the beach, but she reached the rock ahead of him. When he climbed beside her, puffing, she put out her two hands and smoothed his hair.

"Youth ahead of age," he gasped.

"Hush," she said. "I hate young men." And with this she leaned to him and pressed her lips, sweet and salty, against his. He did not move for a long instant, and then he drew back, aghast at the upsurge of desire in his loins.

He woke in the night to the sound of waves beating upon the shore and a strong wind blowing from the south. A gale was rising, and he got up to close the window. What about Elena's room? She slept like a child, deep and undisturbed, and her windows opened to the south. He hesitated, put on his bathrobe, and opened her door softly. The white curtains floated across the room, but she lay motionless on the wide bed beside which the night lamp burned. He shut the windows and then, hesitating again, he leaned over her. She was curled into the pillows, her cheek on her hand, and he was surprised to see the sadness of her face, a child's sadness but a child somehow no longer young. As though aware of his presence she sighed, turned, and flung out her arms. He held his breath, waiting for her eyes to open, but they did not. Instead she sank back into sleep again. Should he wake her? He longed to do so, and dared not, lest he lose control of his life. He knew himself, a man who did not easily love. And what sort of love was this? Partly child love, perhaps love for the daughter he had never had, but more than that, surely if it were anything at all.

He had no illusions about her and wanted none. She was a child in all ways but in the flesh and would be a child as long as she lived, a creature doomed to waywardness and confusion, melancholy and ecstasy. But, and this he faced somberly as he stood looking down on her outflung before him, this was not cause for the upthrust surge of feeling. What he felt was not love of child or woman. A simpler man would simply have taken her for himself. Lust was the word, a good honest word, justified between free man and woman as equals. Yet here there was no equality. He loved his wife and he was too sophisticated, or fastidious, or whatever, to indulge in lust without love. Love-making! He had made good love with Ethel and would again. She was no prude. She understood him, and he knew her. And tempted though he now was, and angry that he could be tempted, and fully aware that he would loathe himself more than he was willing to contemplate, he sighed and tiptoed away. Outside the door it occurred to him that she might have been awake through all his indecision and he opened the door again softly and looked in, half hoping, fool that he was and aware of his folly, that he would see her lying awake, or out of bed, ready to run to him. But she had not moved. Was she honestly asleep or was she just pretending? Suddenly Henry laughed—and he didn't recognize the sound as coming from his own being. This was the laugh of one animal lusting after another animal, primitive, basic, simple. He moved quickly to the bed again and impatiently he flung aside his bathrobe, tore at the buttons on his pajamas and heard the first drops of rain slanting against the windows. Let it rain—let it roar. He laughed again, and with a little shriek Elena tried to sit up. Roughly he pushed her back and knelt above her.

"Henry," she screamed. "You're having a nightmare —you're drunk. Let me go—let me go."

"Let me go, let me go," he mimicked. He grabbed the pillow from behind her head, sank his fingers into her tangled hair, and kicked the sheet aside. Elena began to whimper. "Let me go, you're hurting me. Henry, let me go!"

He pressed his strong muscular thigh between her kicking legs and pinned her so she could not move. Wide-eyed, lips parted, she stared up at him in disbelief.

"That's it, my pretty, look dramatic, act dramatic. Isn't that what Dane teaches you? Give it all you've got. This is a big love scene and you've got to act it out. You've led me on and on like poor Bert and all the other puppets you dangle on your cute little string. Poor old Henry, poor dear, he's rich and safe and fun to tease—"

Elena was crying now and mumbling incoherently. She shook her head from side to side, the great round tears spilling down her cheeks.

"That's it, you beautiful little bitch—cry on cue, cry and I'll lick the salt away." He kissed her harshly, grinding his mouth against hers and he could feel her hands digging into his back, raking with her long fingernails. He shifted slightly, spreading her wide. He was not being gentle and he knew it. Now he wanted to hurt her. He grinned down at her, mocking her, knowing that he was in command and nothing would stop him now—nothing. His heart pounded wildly and he knew that what he was feeling inside was hot, naked lust. The scent of Elena was in his nostrils—earthy, musky, steamy. This little she-cat beneath him had driven him mad. At fifty years old, Henry Potter had been driven mad with lust, a lust he had never before felt!

Nothing could stop him now—nothing. Elena had sunk her teeth into his shoulder. He felt a sharp pain, like a stab wound. She slapped him once, twice, and he felt those cat's claws rake across his neck. He was on fire.

"Henry, I hate you—I love you—I hate you." He heard her, smelled her, tasted her. The weight of his world was on Henry Potter's shoulders and suddenly it crashed around him like the waves crashing on the shore outside. He lay panting, spent. Elena was sobbing softly, huddled in a heap like a frightened child. Henry didn't look at her again. He got up off the bed, picked up his pajamas and bathrobe, and left the room as silently as he had entered it minutes before.

He returned to his own room and showered and changed into fresh pajamas. He then went downstairs to the darkened living room, poured himself a generous portion of cognac, and sank into his easy chair by the window. He put his head back and closed his eyes, savoring the sound of the waves breaking against the shore. The tide would be ebbing, just as the storm was ebbing, and in the morning the world would be calm—calm—calm. Slowly Henry sipped the cognac, letting the liquid roll around on his tongue, feeling the warmth seep down inside himself to the very tips of his fingers, his toes. Only his head felt clear, cool. He drew a long breath. Never, he thought, never, have I been in such complete control. Just as when he had lost control of himself he had been in control of Elena's body, now he was in control of his own body again—his own thoughts, his own soul.

The restlessness and agitation that had burned his

being for the past few weeks were gone—finished. He was once again Henry Potter—he knew what he was doing and where he was going from here. It was odd that he felt no guilt, no remorse. Instead he felt sure of himself. Complete! Yes, that was it! Sure of himself and complete—as Ethel had always felt sure of herself. Ethel, dear, sweet, calm Ethel, with her cool eyes forever observing him, aware of the slightest change in him, yet keeping her distance—respecting his privacy. Damn it, Henry said aloud, why the hell has she so completely respected my privacy. Why has she never asked me what I am thinking or what I am feeling? Instead she just waits and watches with her coolness, her love. What the hell does she expect—what will she expect when we are together again? Would she open her heart to share his passion?

He knew she was passionate because, oh, what the hell—now, this instant, he needed his wife desperately —he wanted to talk, talk, talk—he wanted to explain to her what he had been thinking, feeling, and dreaming. He wanted to make love to her as he had never before made love to anyone.

Fool, Henry accused himself—old fool. Afraid of your own wife, and where is she now when you need her—off wandering somewhere alone. Alone? With a pang of unaccustomed jealousy, Henry wondered if she *was* alone and if she was yearning for him as he was yearning for her. Maybe she had taken a lover, maybe . . . oh, God, Henry groaned and downed his cognac with a gulp. He set the glass aside and it clattered unnoticed to the floor. He let his arms dangle loosely over the sides of the chair. Ethel, Ethel—why aren't you here now when I need you? And Elena upstairs! What of her? Is she still crying? Is she miserable? No, thought Henry, of course she's not miserable. To her their earlier moments had been merely an incident, just a scene, just an act. Well, aren't we all actors?

He stood up, suddenly impatient for the dawn to come. He saw his own reflection in the mirror above the fireplace, and in the reflection in the background the waves rolled in and subsided over the sandy beach. In the half-light his own face looked back at him, revealing his inner self to him for the first time. You are also an actor, he told the face in the mirror— you're no better than Elena. You are but an actor, on life's stage. Oh, trite words, he sneered. Admit to yourself, Henry Potter, you were getting dissatisfied with Ethel and yourself and everything else in your life. Marie staring at you every day with her hang-dog expression, employees expecting you to be the same day after day, meetings, dinners, Ethel constantly insisting you go to the theater. Ah yes, the theater.

Abruptly Henry turned and faced the sea. I'm like Dane. A director. I want to direct—I *want* to direct my own life. I inherited my name, my business, my social standing. Who would I be if I were not Henry Potter? He smiled at the absurd wanderings of his thoughts. Fool, he chided himself again. Old fool. Tomorrow—yes, tomorrow—I'll call Ethel in Rio and tell her to come home where she belongs, and I'll tell her everything—about myself, about the play, the people, and she will understand. Oh, yes, Ethel will understand. She knows me, by God, he told himself, she knows me, and all this time she's been waiting for me to know myself!

Morning would come and he would face Elena as if nothing had happened. Elena, the actress, Elena, the star of the play, *his* play. She will be a success, she will be a star. The play will go on, it will be a success—maybe not a great play, but a good play, and

I will be proud of my part in it. You'll see, Ethel, you'll see. Ethel, I need you, I want you! He was filled with desire, with longing—impatient for morning to come.

In the evening, in the last hours before they must return to the city, they sat before the fire. The day had been wet and cool and the house was damp. Out of the sea, mists rose and covered the beach and the lawns and crept over the roof. She had insisted, nevertheless, on dashing into the icy water, and he had stood on the sand, anxious until he saw her emerge. At dinner she had been strangely silent, looking at him with questioning eyes. He had tried to make her smile, or even to speak, telling her tales of his boyhood here, and how he had once been marooned upon the tide-washed rocks. She had listened without hearing, and after they had finished they went to the living room and he lit the fire, and sat himself by it, with his coffee, which she refused because she said it was bitter, a Brazilian brew, clear and strong, that he and Ethel liked. She had stood uncertain for a moment, eyes upon him in the unfathomable and causeless melancholy that was part of her nature. Then she had dropped to the floor and now sat leaning against him, still silent, her head against his knees. He gave up trying to talk, and then happening to glance from the fire to her, he saw her licking the palm of her hand with the tip of her tongue.

"What are you—a pussy cat?"

"I like the taste of myself."

She put up her hand. "Taste!"

And feeling silly and shy, he put out his tongue and touched the smooth fine skin with his tongue.

"Salt," he said. "You didn't wash off the sea when you came in."

"I never wash it off," she said. "I stay salty with sea water. It feels good."

She sat licking her palm with small touches of her tongue tip, as unselfconscious as a young animal. And yet he suspected shrewdly that she was never purely unselfconscious. Whatever she did, the actress assumed the pose of a simplicity he doubted but which charmed him, nevertheless. As though she divined his doubt, she stopped, and folding her hands, she sat gazing into the fire.

"You don't feel like talking?" he asked.

"What is there to talk about?"

"Nothing, if you have nothing to say."

"I'm happy," she said. "I'm just happy. I love you. I want you to know. I love you better than anybody in the world." She turned to him impetuously and knelt before him, her arms folded on his knees. "No, I simply don't love anybody else."

He looked down into the warm and lovely face, and could have believed her. His body trembled but he was suddenly cooled again by a strange humility, new to him. This young and exquisite creature so to address him, an aging man!

"Thank you," he said at last, his voice husky.

She sank back on her heels and stared at him.

"Is that all you have to say? Just 'thank you,' as though I'd handed you a cup of tea?"

To his amazement, she was ready to be angry. "But Elena——"

"You don't love me."

She leaped to her feet. He was appalled at the fury in her eyes. Then he had an inspiration. "Elena, I wish you could see yourself. I shall never forget the way you look at this moment. You are a very great actress."

She wavered, she walked two steps toward him and stopped, her face like a flower waiting for rain. He went on.

"I've never been quite sure, you know. But now I'm sure. I want you to be sure, too—of yourself."

He put out his arms and she ran into them and clung to him, weeping. "Oh, Henry, how did you know what to say? Do you think I'm great? I mean really great—not just—"

"Not just beautiful," he said gently.

She pulled herself out of his arms. "Because I hate just being beautiful."

"Ah now, don't hate yourself!"

"Because that's all men see—that I'm beautiful. And I want to be great—great—great!" She pounded her breast with her clenched fists.

Ah, how he had been saved! If he had yielded now to the organic desire, the universal attraction, he would have lost her and himself. She did not want him, or any man, except for a moment, perhaps, and no more. She was touched with genius and he knew the ruthlessness of genius. He had seen it in scientists and artists and—let it be faced—even in himself. Ethel had accused him once, years ago, of not being able to love her whole because he loved something more than he could love any human being. And he had acknowledged that it was so.

"At least," he had said, "I love you as much as I can love anyone."

And she had accepted him, as he well knew, upon that basis. "Very well," she had said. "I'll settle for what I can get. . . . Because I do love you—altogether." He had never seen her angry again, nor sad, nor joyful.

Something of that acceptance, or that resignation, crept into his soul now, like the mist from the sea.

Elena had forgotten him. She stood gazing into the dying fire, her cheeks flushed. What was she thinking about? Not, he was sure, about him. At this vantage point of middle age, he could view his own longings with something like amusement, as well as a deep and rueful pain.

He got up from his chair.

"I feel a little tired," he said. "I think I'll say goodnight, my dear."

He reached for his coffee cup on the small table beside him, but the coffee was cold and he put the cup down again. She had not heard him. He left her there smiling into the fire, seeing what visions of herself he did not know.

5

He returned the next morning to his own kingdom with determination undershot by a vague loneliness. This theater business was an aberration, a diversion, and so he would consider it from now on.

He pressed the button for Marie. It was nine o'clock, and when she came in, he asked irritably, "What are you doing with your hat still on? Take it off and bring in the mail. This office is going to pieces."

"I'm glad you see it, Mr. Potter," she retorted. "I've done my best but you're the boss and you've been away most of the time for the last three weeks——"

"Don't stand there chattering."

She disappeared, her eyes suddenly red, and he sat grimly waiting, his hands clenched into fists on his desk.

She was back almost immediately with Monday's mail, always formidable, and began talking as she opened the door.

"Two of the directors have died in the last week— Mr. Frederics and Mr. Slattery. Both over eighty, and——"

"I've been waiting for that," he said. "Did you send flowers?"

"Roses to one, lilies to the other."

"Those two stubborn old men gone! They always wanted to manage the company—as though a bunch of directors ever knows what's going on in the works!

Amateurs! I want some men as good as I am, who'll know enough to criticize me when I need it."

She put the letters before him. "That's what you say, Mr. Potter, but I don't believe you'd like it, actually. I've never known you to like being criticized."

He read as he talked. "Depends on who does it. I've got a good mind to put in two of our own men."

"They won't dare criticize you, Mr. Potter. They'll be afraid you'd fire them."

He snorted laughter. "Pity you're only a woman, Marie! You're never afraid. Well, what's the proportion now?"

"If you filled the two vacancies with outside men, it would be two outside to one inside."

"Maybe that's about right. Yes, I guess so. . . . Now get to work."

"Yes, Mr. Potter."

He dictated steadily for two hours and then, alone for ten minutes before his junior executives came in for a conference, he could not resist calling the theater.

"Aubrey Dane," he said to the operator, and waited irritably and with a pounding heart for five full minutes, resolved not to mention Elena.

"Hello." Dane's voice was dangerously soft and cool.

"How are things going?" he asked.

"All right."

"No problems?"

"Not more than usual."

Damn the fellow, there was only one problem—Elena.

"Big problems?"

"We have no theater yet."

"He promised."

"You can't go on a promise in this business, Mr. Potter. You have to have a contract."

"Tell him to give us a contract."

"Vallant is on a cruise."

"There must be somebody who can act for him."

"Nobody that seems to want to—they are afraid of our play."

"What do you mean, afraid of our play?"

"Not enough sex in it—not enough violence. I've been through all this before."

"What idiotic stuff—what do you mean?"

"And it's not a musical."

"So?"

"So it ought to have sixty percent sex and forty percent violence or vice versa, to be sure box office."

"What kind of talk is that?"

"That's what they say."

"I'm coming to the theater."

"I wish you would."

He slammed down the receiver and sat impatiently through an hour's conference and on the way to the theater conceived, out of anger, a notion which he knew was extravagance and instantly decided upon it because it was exciting. How dare a man go on a cruise without keeping his promise? He would buy a theater. He could thenceforth be independent of all unreliable theater characters. He lowered the glass panel between himself and the driver.

"Beaman, stop at Jones and Johnson. Real estate—you remember?"

"Yes, sir."

He got out of the car ten minutes later and rode an elevator to the thirtieth floor and entered the real estate offices of Jones and Johnson, who had obtained for him the block of old buildings upon whose site he had built his glass palace.

"No, I have no appointment," he told the new silver blonde at the desk. "Just say it's Henry Potter."

"Yes, sir."

He stood while she telephoned, and in a moment Chetham Jones came out to greet him. He was a short, square man with a salesman's smile and small intelligent gray eyes.

"Mr. Potter, what a pleasure—"

"I should have let you know I was coming, but an idea struck me on the way downtown."

"Come in, always glad to see you."

He followed the neatly fat figure who led the way to the innermost office, decorated in severe brown and white modern furniture.

"I want to buy a theater, Chet, and buy it now."

"A theater, Mr. Potter? Sit down."

Chetham Jones sat down, not behind the desk, but in an easy chair, in the approved new manner for executives, designed to put customers at ease.

"A theater," Henry Potter said, "and I have a special reason for wanting something now."

Jones pursed his small plump mouth. "I don't know of a theater unless you want to buy an old motion picture house. It could be renovated."

"How long would that take?"

"Six months or so—rush job."

"Too late! I want to use the theater in four weeks. Buy something that's ready."

"I'd have to persuade somebody to sell, Mr. Potter. I don't know that anybody does want to sell. Business is good now, and every house is booked."

"Well, persuade somebody. You can always find something if you offer enough."

Chetham Jones coughed behind his small fat left

hand, decorated with a gold wedding ring. "Am I to understand that money is no deterrent?"

"None, if you can get it in time for the opening of a play, four weeks from now."

"A play, Mr. Potter?"

"A play." He rose to his feet. "That's all I came for, Chet, and I'll expect to hear from you before the day is over."

"I'll get right to work, Mr. Potter. You'll hear something by five o'clock."

"I don't want to hear something. I want to hear that I own a theater."

"Well, I hope—"

"Don't say you hope. Say you'll do it."

Chetham Jones laughed uncomfortably. "I don't like to—"

"Yes, you do. You'll just love the big fat commission you'll get."

He went away, feeling dissatisfied but undefeated. He would get a theater somehow. He got into the car again and a few minutes later was at the theater.

"Beaman, pick me up here at five o'clock," he said, and went in, prepared to face crisis.

But the atmosphere in the theater was one of peace and restrained excitement. Elena was playing the scene of Jennet's awakening, the moment when her lover, not yet accepted, reveals that her husband is working on an invention which may, if it falls in the wrong hands, destroy an entire people. This woman, herself escaped from a defeated country, sheltered finally in what she imagines a safe land, a secure house, a beloved husband, faces a future dependent upon the dedicated mind of a scientist. Where is her refuge now?

Elena was playing with superb and delicate skill the tremulous intensity of a woman reluctant to be awakened to the harshness of facts she feared to know. He had been wrong about Elena. She was not a child. She was a woman, mature, loyal, reasoning, intuitive, reluctant to yield to a new love and yet unable to refuse, lest her only personal security be in love. And then the perception, growing out of her own mind, disclosed to her that even personal security was none at all, unless it were part of the total security of every individual being everywhere. In such predicament, where could she find safety except in taking those same facts, one by one, and facing them, a woman awakened at last to reality?

He watched her upon the stage growing from a child, woman, wife, mother of a child, absorbed in her small organic life, to a human being who was at last a woman, and he was shocked and half ashamed to find tears in his eyes. How nearly he had come to making this growth impossible! For what would have happened to Elena if he had diverted her to himself, and thus had wasted this precious gift which she expended so effortlessly here upon the stage? Her voice, her every gesture, the way she walked, were no longer those of Elena. She was that other woman, or any woman, caught in new circumstances.

He felt a touch on his sleeve. Stella Dane had moved to the seat beside him to whisper at his ear.

"She's got it at last! She's stopped fighting the part. She's in it. I wonder what happened."

"She's not afraid any more. She knows she can do it," he whispered back. He glanced at her curiously. "How does it feel?"

"Feel?"

"To see the woman you made come to flesh and blood up there."

"It's a miracle. It's like seeing a statue come to life.

. . . Pygmalion! Simply a miracle! I can't criticize yet, not until it ceases to be a miracle just to see her move and hear her speak. Aubrey says I'll get over it and start picking her to pieces. I can't believe him."

He had never heard the quiet woman talk so much, nor before seen her face come alive and lose its closed calm. It occurred to him that he was also learning something about women. Long ago he had read somewhere that if a man knew one woman whole he knew every woman. What of Ethel? Perhaps he had never known her—something of Stella, something of Elena, in the mixture of Ethel. It had never occurred to him to consider the composition of the female mind. After half a century of life wholly in masculine terms, perhaps it was even too late. At this moment a wisp of knowledge floated out of his memory. His education had given him no coordinated body of such knowledge and yet as a preparation for efficiency he had acquired the habit of cohesive thought. The wisp just now was a famous event in the life of the English philosopher, Hobbes. He had come upon it when he was in college, cramming for a test, long forgotten except for the unrelated fact. Hobbes was forty years old before he looked at geometry, and then he did so by the chance of seeing a geometry book open upon a friend's table. Idly he read the 47th Proposition of Euclid. My God, he had thought, that could not be true, and then he looked back to the axiom upon which it depended, and so to the very beginning of the book and thereby his whole life was changed. The universe, which he had supposed was static, immovable, solid, he now perceived was constant only in motion. Table, chair, house, the structures of physical life, were trembling, jumping, alive with the energy of motion and change. "When a body is once in motion," Hobbes had declared, "it moveth, unless something else hinder it, eternally."

Was he, Henry Potter, not also a body?

"And what is the heart, but a spring," Hobbes had inquired. "And what are the nerves but so many springs, and the joints, but so many wheels, giving motion to the whole body?"

It was Hobbes who had defined causality—no effect without cause.

He turned to the quiet woman at his side. "Will you have lunch with me?"

Stella Dane turned to him in surprise. "Oh—why? You needn't, you know. I'm not Elena."

"I would enjoy it, if you are free."

"I am always free," she said.

The imperturbable Beaman waiting outside had apparently come to take for granted this change in his employer's life. He was reading a paperback book entitled *Stars and Atoms,* and he put it down to leap from his seat and open the door.

"Where to, sir?"

"The Plaza," Henry Potter said. He took his seat beside the quiet woman.

"Do you take Elena to the Plaza?" she inquired with the least possible smile.

"No," he said, "but that is where I would like to go with you."

She did not reply, but he saw her smile deepen. She had a fine profile, he discovered, delicately suntanned skin, and clearly marked black brows. Her hair was straight and dark and long, brushed back from her forehead and knotted not too low at the back.

"Are you a theater person?" he inquired.

"No," she said. "I'm only married to it. I am a writer. As you know, it's my first play."

"Then you can tell me—are they what I think they are?"

"What do you think they are?"

"A peculiar breed of children. My wife and I went to Africa once, on one of those safari things. Part of the journey lay through a belt of rain forest in the heart of the continent and there we saw pigmies— strange children, with old faces. They lived in their own world, they mated and bore other children, they went through all the gestures of life, but it was not life as I knew it and in an inexplicable way they weren't people. Somewhere along the way between childhood and adulthood they had simply stopped. Everything they did seemed like play. They lived at play. They weren't playful—that's the odd thing about it. They weren't playful. And these people in the theater—they aren't playful. Children are never playful. It's only the very wise, the very superior people, who are playful."

She turned her pale classic face to him and said as though it were poetry, something he remembered to have heard someone read aloud in English for his benefit in the ashram at Almora.

Steady in the state of fullness which shines
when all desires are given up, and peaceful
in the state of freedom in life, act playfully
in the world!

Inwardly free from all desires, dispassionate
and detached, but outwardly active in all
directions, act playfully in the world!

Free from egoism, but with mind detached as
in sleep, pure like the sky, ever untainted, act
playfully in the world!

Conducting yourself nobly with kindly
   tenderness,
outwardly conforming to conventions but
   inwardly
renouncing all, act playfully in the world!

Quite unattached at heart but for all appearance
acting as with attachment, inwardly cool, but
outwardly full of fervor, act playfully in the
world!

When she had repeated these lines she turned her
face away again.

"I heard those words long ago in India," he said.

"I have never been in India," she said, "but once
I read the words in a book and I say them to myself
every morning when I wake to face the day and again
when in bed I face the night."

And then suddenly with a sort of passion she be-
sought him. "Please never be impatient with Aubrey!
He will disappoint you again and again, inevitably,
sometime, somewhere. You will expect him to be wise,
and he will not be wise. You will expect him to respond
to some feeling you may have for him, but he will not
respond. You will hope for something from him, but
he will never give it."

He was sorely embarrassed at all this and he stam-
mered in his effort to reply, "What could I want from
him?"

She answered with a strange, sad conviction. "Oh,
you will want something from him—everyone does.
But he will never give it. Do you know why? Because
he has only one world—his own, and it is in the
theater. There he lives his half life, and he directs
other people to live their half lives."

He had a sudden perception of why her eyes were sorrowful. "Is that why you wrote a play? For him?"

She nodded. "How else can we ever meet?" She was silent for a moment and then she said, "I go into his world since he cannot enter mine—because I love him."

Never before had he made such deep talk with a human being he did not know.

"Why do you love him?"

"I don't know."

"Is it love?"

"As much as my blood and bones and heart and breathing are part of me."

"And your mind?"

"My mind lives alone. There is no communication between our minds."

"And you still call it love?"

She flung out her hands. "As much as this body is me."

He pondered this soberly. A few weeks ago he would not have known what she was talking about, but now he knew.

"Will it last?"

"Who knows?" she replied. "But it is all I have."

They had finished their meal, and he rose to move her chair and though they had scarcely spoken through the half hour, he leaned over to put one final question: "What do you do until you know?"

She flashed him a brilliant upward glance. "I wait," she said. "I wait—and I act playfully!"

He followed her out of the crowded room, and was well aware of her distinction as heads turned to watch her tall grace. She herself looked neither to the right nor to the left, a superb woman, he told himself, and yet not many men would love her. A few, but those few would be worth knowing. He was suddenly filled with intense curiosity about her, without the slightest stir of the blood. Concerning Elena he had felt no curiosity whatever, and nothing but the stir. He was ashamed now that his mind, in sudden secret inquiry, wondered if this woman were passionate. He knew she was, but only to the few, or perhaps only to the one, and why was Aubrey Dane that one? To which his astute mind replied that he ought to know, for let him put the same question to himself and the answer was clear, a curious equation, she was to Aubrey Dane as he was to Elena, whatever that was—

Out of the fog of human emotion whose elements bewildered him, so involved had he become with this handful of strangers among whom he now spent most of his waking hours, the play began to emerge with a life of its own. It was a life closed to him, the spectator, a microcosm in which Aubrey Dane was the father and the creator, and the actors his creatures. They were dependent upon Dane, supported and enlivened by his praise, crushed by his disapproval. He was absorbed in them and by them, unseeing, deaf to all others. They had become his children, his flesh, his blood. His touch upon them was intimate, he manipulated them, adjusting their costumes, directing the arrangement of Elena's hair, and then, pushing away the hairdresser, brushing her straight, long hair himself. He applied the streaks of gold as carefully as though she were indeed his child, and she bent her head, leaning her cheek against his breast. When he had the effect he wished, he took her head in his hands.

"Beautiful, my beautiful," he murmured, and kissed her forehead.

At such a moment Henry Potter glanced at the silent

woman who sat beside him in the empty theater, day after day. Stella turned her head slightly to catch the edge of his glance and smiled.

"Never mind," he muttered.

"What good does it do to mind? He is living his own life but at least he's alive."

"You gave it to him, didn't you? Writing the play—"

"Yes, I suppose so."

"Aren't you to blame?"

"No. He'd find it somewhere else with someone else. Then I'd have nothing of him. He's not happy except when he's directing."

"Do you do it only for him?"

"No. Yes, perhaps I do. I don't know."

"What would you be doing if you'd never met him?"

"I can't imagine."

"Then he gives you something, too, in his own fashion."

"A sort of life," she said. "A half life—"

"Playing at life?"

"Acting playfully, we live," she agreed.

He let it go at that. Besides, the play was now a shape, a world in itself, not yet plain, but struggling to arrive at clarity. Dane was wrestling with it, trying the actors this way and that, torturing words, changing lines. Again and again he strode to the edge of the stage and shouted into the twilight.

"Stella!"

"Here," she called back, always immediate.

"Cut last two lines from Jerome's speech on page thirty-seven?"

"I'm all for cuts. . . ."

". . . Stella!"

"Yes, Aubrey?"

"I want a love word—not love, but another word—

no, not 'adore,' not anything hackneyed—something fresh—"

"Is there a word for love that's fresh?"

"Must be—must be. Think—can't you think?"

"Thinking won't do it—"

"Well, *feel* then! Where's your imagination?"

"What about 'crave'?"

He tasted the word on his tongue. " 'Crave'? 'Crave'? We'll try it—try anything. Maybe that's all love is, anyway—craving. All right—crave! It's repulsive, sort of—but maybe that's all right, too. . . . Henry! I'm leaving the theater to you. I'm leaving everything else but the play to you."

"Sure," Henry Potter said.

He stayed to see the first complete run-through of the play, to the end, the doubtful, troublesome end, which still was not right and would perhaps never be right, for how could a cosmic question, asked in a shack in a desert, find its answer? Is it or is it not worthwhile for a woman to bear children and make a shack into a home, when the man who fathers those children is at the same time creating an instrument for total destruction of the race? Who was to save her by answering the question? It did not yet occur to her to find her own answer.

Upon the stage Jennet, who was Elena, turned blindly to the younger man, poet as well as scientist, musician as well as man.

"Oh, Mark, Mark, who will save me?"

"Not I," he said. "I cannot save myself." And he left her.

Alone, the woman in the desert lifted her face to the empty sky, to make her demand. "Why should a woman create a child nowadays? To what end?"

The answer was silence. In silence the play was ended.

Henry Potter turned to Stella. "You can't leave it like that. There has to be an answer, something that satisfies the audience."

"Oh," she whispered, "don't you see? None of us has the answer. We keep dreaming up these rainbows— pots of gold beyond the horizon—that's all any play can be. No woman will ever be Jennet, really. She's only the woman we'd like to be—brave enough to question life!"

"Go home, Stella," he said. "Go home and stay by yourself until you have found an answer."

She stared at him. "Are you serious?"

"Of course I am. You've written a play without an end. But there has to be an end. You've keyed everybody up to crisis, and then you don't face the crisis. You can't slip out of it. What will you do? You have to tell us. Else there's no play—it's all meaningless."

She cried out at him. "God himself can't answer the question! So he just—makes an end to people. *Be silent,* he says, and he squashes us back into the dust. That's why there has to be death. Else there'd be no end. Shall I kill everybody off, too?"

"That's not good enough for a play," he said grimly. "Who wants to see something that's no better than life? Go home and think up something. Meanwhile, I'll get a theater for you—you and your rainbow."

He stood up and as though she were in a daze she too got to her feet and went away. He found Beaman outside in the car waiting and asleep with a newspaper over his face, and he woke him and drove to his office and called Sidney Vallant. A nasal voice answered and he recognized the possessor as the dyed blonde at the reception desk.

"Mr. Vallant? He's gone on a cruise—Mediterranean—and won't be back for three months. Who'd you say you were?"

"Henry Potter."

"Oh, Mr. Potter—wait a minute, please!"

Some kind of talk went on, and then he heard a hoarse voice which again he recognized as emanating from the fat man.

"Mr. Potter?"

"Yes—"

"Mr. Vallant said you could have the first theater where the play flops. That'll be one on Forty-sixth—the Kramer comedy, *Sing a Song of Sunshine*. Not funny. I give it six days. Course, something might happen to make it hold on a few days more—"

"I'll sign a contract now."

"Better wait—it's not legal yet."

"We'll make it contingent."

He sent Marie for the contract and he signed it and told Aubrey Dane that night.

"Good," Aubrey said indifferently. "It's not the best, but it will do. By the way—model of the set will be here tomorrow."

The model stood upon a small table at the left of the stage, an exquisite miniature of the desert and the house. Cactus grew by the doorway and a small swimming pool shimmering blue and silvery paint lay under a tree. He gazed at the scene, charmed by its tiny beauty, its imitation of reality—no, its imitation of an imitation, related to the play as the play was related to life.

Aubrey Dane strolled toward it and the actors followed like children to stand in a semicircle, listening as he talked. "Here's where action begins, here's where

Jennet enters. White bathing suit. She's just been swimming, and she calls the children. She has no idea of what's ahead for her so she's all happiness and light—eh, Elena?—and she thinks she's a good wife and mother and she doesn't want to be anything else. Here, to the left, is where the man comes in, husband to her, father to her children. Oh, she knows he's a scientist, a world-famous person and all that, but it's not important to her. *He's* important. He's her world. She chose him, years before, when she was in England.

"But a woman never quite forgets a man who's been in love with her. It's always in her, an embryo. So when Jerome invites Mark, now the brilliant young English nuclear physicist, to come to the secret laboratory in the desert to help him solve a snag he's struck —remember to call it *laboratry*, Bert—he doesn't know that he's unlocking a closed door in his wife's heart— get that, Elena! The first minute Marks walks in I want you to convey to the audience that you remember every minute you spent with him, walking the lanes of England, lying on the grass of a summer's evening in Hyde Park, and so on. You thought you'd forgotten but you haven't."

"Shall I be scared?" Elena asked.

"Don't ask me," Dane retorted. "You know! If you don't know, then you haven't learned your part."

"I am scared," Elena said, "but it's—delicious!"

"All right! Don't interrupt again, please! Attention, children!" He turned to face the cast. "Chess says some of you are coming in late again. I won't stand for it. We're dangerously near D-day. Now, Elena, sweetheart, the big love scene again, please. Quiet on the stage, everybody!"

They scattered like happy children. The blonde understudy for Elena settled herself with three other actors in their unending game of poker at which she won steadily day after day. Elena and Bert stood in the center of the stage and went through a few exercises, neither paying heed to the other.

Dane spoke sharply. "All right, Jennet, take your position. Mark, you've just had your big scene with Jerome. You've told him that you won't help him unless you know what the invention is for. . . . Jerome! Stand in position for his last lines."

Jerome, the tall gray-haired actor, took his place at a door. Mark straightened himself, clenched his fists, and shouted, "I have a right to know what you are using my brains for! I have a responsibility to myself! I'll ask you once more—are you making a weapon?"

Jerome answered softly, reasonably.

"It could be a weapon, Mark, but it needn't be. It all depends on who uses it."

The lines flowed smoothly on.

"Ah, that's it! Who's to use it? I have a right to know."

"Don't be absurd, Mark. We scientists have only one responsibility: to pursue knowledge. We can't be responsible for what other people do with the knowledge."

"Then we are immoral—"

"Neither moral nor immoral."

"I won't help you, Jerome."

"Look here, Mark—there'd never have been any scientific progress if we'd all taken your stand—what about fire? Suppose the first firemaker had stopped because some fool idealist said it could kill people—"

"I won't help you, Jerome, unless I know who will be in control of my brains."

"Exit Jerome," Dane said. "Now then, lovers—Mark, watch me."

He stepped forward and walked to face Elena. He was no longer Aubrey Dane. He was a young, uncertain, defiant scientist, a troubled genius, an angry boy.

"Jennet! Am I wrong?"

She shook her head, gazed into his eyes, parted her lips to speak and did not speak, the lovely mouth open like a rose.

He came nearer to her, he seized her shoulders. "I haven't to sell myself, you know! It isn't as though I were poor or struggling or anything like that. I've my own laboratories in England, you know. I left an immensely important research I'm doing on my own. I'm taking up the unified field where Einstein left off. And I don't propose to work on a damned machine that could be used by rascals! How has it come about that Jerome allows himself to work on such a machine?"

"I don't know anything about it, Mark."

"But you should know something about it, Jennet! That's the trouble with women. You potter about with your houses and babies and never ask whether some man is about to destroy the whole thing—no, that's not fair of me. Why do I suddenly call you 'women'—as though you were all the women in the world—which you are to me, more than ever. . . . Jennet, it was because of you that I came!"

"Back away now, Jennet," Dane muttered under his breath. "Don't just stand there. You see what's coming. You want to be loyal to your husband. You don't want me—ah, you do want me! Get that look into your eyes. Concentrate on sex. You know how to do it. I'm coming nearer. Relax your muscles. Your blood is rushing through your body. You feel limp. You remember what you thought you'd forgotten—how I kissed you. Not every man knows how to kiss a woman. This man does.

That's right, my sweetheart! That's the look I want. Your lips parted, my darling—"

He put his palms on her cheeks, he lifted her head, and slowly he kissed her full on the mouth, a long kiss, his hands slipping down her neck, over her shoulders, clasping her close from shoulder to knee.

In the surrounding twilight Henry Potter was suddenly aware of Stella. She had come in silently and unseen. He stole a look at her. She sat motionless, her eyes on her hands folded on her knees.

"What does this kind of thing do to a woman's husband?" he muttered.

She looked up with a smile too bright. "Aubrey? Oh, it's quite all right. He's a woman's director, you know. It's his technique. Haven't you noticed? Gentle voice, courteous, always considerate, delicate, the technique of lovemaking, you know. Devotion centered upon the one woman, little touches seemingly so innocent, apparently so instinctive, compliments, 'Your hands are so beautiful'—'Your skin, darling, like rose leaves'—'Why don't I have a smile like yours, sweetheart?' "

Her voice was Aubrey's to an echo. He could have laughed except that suddenly she turned her head away.

"So those words don't mean a thing to you, when he says them to you."

"I hate them," she said. Her voice was cold and soft. "I never let him speak them to me. Keep them, I tell him, keep them for your showgirls!"

He was aghast at the wound he had opened. "Why can't I keep my mouth shut?"

"No, no! I'm glad—it does me good. I haven't anyone to talk to. It's I who am confused—not him. He doesn't love anybody, really. He's vain—of course he's vain. He can't pass a mirror without looking at himself.

Have you ever noticed? But I love him . . . God knows why. I have no reason to—"

"You mean—"

"I simply mean that he doesn't know how to love anybody. Oh, sex, yes—plenty of that, but not with love. Not at all."

She pushed back her hair with sudden violence. "I've had to—well, why don't I tell you? Who cares?"

"You mean he—"

"No, I don't mean he sleeps with these girls of his. Maybe he does. I don't know. It's more honest if he does, at that."

"More honest than—"

"More honest than coming home at midnight all stirred up and pretending that I'm the girl. Look here, I tell him. I'm me, myself, your wife. I'm not Elena or Jennet or . . . or . . . or . . . so just don't *use* me!"

He was appalled. Did anyone hear her? No. On the stage Aubrey Dane was placing Bert into the position of embrace. He stepped back, examined the effect, stepped forward and moved Elena's arm.

"Don't clutch him—you're afraid, remember, but you can't stop yourself. Your hand steals ever so slowly along his cheek, your fingers, now your fingers—touching his lips—that's right—creeping down to his neck—slipping under his shirt—open one more button, Mark—that's better. Your fingers, Jennet!"

The actors were watching now, half hidden in the shadows of backstage. Even the card players turned their heads.

"Now," Dane said, "now the kiss!"

Henry Potter looked away. Don't use me! The words so fiercely whispered beside him recalled another voice, another scene, a reality in the night, a night in Paris, a spring night, when Ethel had spoken the words and to him. They had been to see a picture—what was it? *Hiroshima, Mon Amour*. He had been deeply moved by it, the two lovers alone in a strange city, the passion of loneliness mingled with the passion of love. He had yearned for Ethel in the night and she had repulsed him with a fury he had never seen in her, had not suspected was hers.

"Don't touch me!"

"Ethel, what's—"

"Simply don't touch me, that's all. Don't *use* me!"

The memory was unbearable. He got to his feet and tiptoed out of the theater. Those people up there on the stage, those childish, shallow people, not one of whom knew anything about real love or real anything, had nevertheless some uncanny inexplicable instinctive power not to touch reality or to portray anything real in life, but to mirror it so that real people, looking at the dim reflection, saw themselves.

Damn, he'd forgotten that horrible night! When was Ethel coming home? He'd send a cable tomorrow. When in hell are you coming home to me, Ethel? I don't like these people.

He heard her voice, an echo, "Don't use me, Henry!"

He went back, nevertheless. He was back again the next day. His offices, his home seemed empty, the air stagnant, himself meaningless. Even Beaman had looked at him last night at his lonely dinner table and had coughed behind his hand.

"Pardon the mention, sir, but if I may say so, Mrs. Potter being absent, you're not looking well, sir. We've all noticed it."

"I'm well enough," he had grunted. What business had the fellow to notice his looks?

"It's sitting in that theater, sir. I know what it's like."

Henry Potter put down his knife and fork. Beaman backed away from his stare. "Pardon again, sir. I've never told you I was once an actor myself—not that I'd care to have it mentioned. I wasn't important."

Henry Potter took up his knife and fork again. The roast was excellent.

"What's an actor doing as a butler?" he asked. Beaman was slicing the roast in thin pink curls.

"I was a butler on the stage, sir, nearly always. I know the obsession. Try as I would, I couldn't get better parts, and yet I couldn't tear myself away from the theater. My mother was a chorus girl until she married my father. He was a stagehand then. She gave up her career, if you could call it that, but she hankered for it and she had me on the stage as a child, sir, though I had no talent. It got me just the same. So I know the color you get in the theater, sir. Pasty. You do have it, sir, if you'll excuse me. And the young woman you took to the beach, sir, it's none of my business, but I know the type and Mrs. Potter being away—"

Henry Potter lifted his head and looked at the man. He might have been angry but he was only mildly amused. There was something touching about that narrow face flushed now with embarrassment, diffidence, an English awareness of stepping out of his place.

"Well? Go on, Beaman. This is interesting. You want to save me from something? Very good of you! But you'd better tell me what."

"Sir, I can only tell you what about her."

"Sit down, Beaman."

"No, sir, thank you. Please—let me stay in character. Sir, I was wrecked by a woman like her. You'll laugh, since I had nothing better than small parts in any play. But I might have had better if I hadn't followed her everywhere—as I did. At first I thought she was in love with me. She was younger than I—

"I imagined, with the folly of love, that she would leave the stage for me. I hated it all by that time, the corruption combined with the amazing instinct for using the emotions that hide in us all. Perhaps it's that combination that keeps us all enthralled. I'd no more go to the theater, now, Mr. Potter, than I'd take poison. It's like trying to break off drinking, the constant titillation of the senses, the incessant handling of the secret parts in our natures. We go back for it again and again. We say we go for amusement, but it's sorry amusement, destructive amusement, if we were only honest enough to face ourselves and why we do it. Corruption calls to corruption, the corruption that's in us, the elements of the animal. And this—this actress—I won't call her a woman, but she had the shape of woman— she was not stupid. She had a terrifying corrupt cleverness. She applied her whole mind to the study of her own female body and the male instinct. She knew every turn and twist of the muscles in her flesh which would reveal her sex to arouse that instinct in any man. Call it sex appeal? It was torture for any man, anywhere in the world, Indian, African, English, Russian, men who couldn't exchange a word with her. For that matter, she couldn't even speak decent English—she was Cockney born and bred. But she didn't need to speak. She communicated with the lowest and men followed her like idiots. The very smell of her—what am I saying?"

"I know what you mean," Henry Potter said.

"It's because I know that you know that I'm saying all this. For she could reduce any man to the same level. I can't mention names, of course, but you'd know the names of the men if I spoke them—intellectual men, men dedicated to their country or to some great cause, men of great families. She married seven times, always to a great man! Of course she never married me. She looked at me for a few days at first, when she'd just crawled out of the gutter, because I was in a position to do something for her—then."

The man's lips trembled. He was a handsome fellow, Henry Potter observed anew, not much above forty.

"The horrible fact is that I forgive her," he was saying. "I know—or I comprehend somehow—that she couldn't help being what she was. I know that she could never love anyone. She was cold. Love was not in her. Not even lust was in her. Her lust was all toward herself. She petted her own beautiful body, she adored herself. She showed herself off and men went mad. She was in a continual rut. They didn't even want her for themselves. They wanted to drown themselves in her, join her adoration of her body, become part of her own orgy, lose themselves in her animal being. And that's what she wanted, too. She took them. They never took her. They wanted to be consumed by her. They wanted to be passive while she destroyed them. They were delirious with death. When she threw them aside they were too weak to suffer. There was nothing left in them. She had taken their manhood for her own use, and she was strong—strong—strong—you know those savages who eat their enemies so they can grow the stronger?"

Henry Potter looked down at his plate. The conversation was horrifying in its reality. The fellow was an actor, of course. He mustn't forget that. Nevertheless, he knew now what the fellow meant and a few weeks ago he wouldn't have known. He would merely have thought the fellow was mad. He put his knife and fork together neatly and wiped his lips on the big old-fashioned linen napkins that Ethel always provided.

"I don't know that I can think of you as a butler any more, Beaman."

The man laughed unsteadily. "Please try, sir. Else I shall have to give notice."

Henry Potter drank the last of his coffee. "You prefer to be a butler and chauffeur?"

"It's a quiet life, sir. No emotional upsets."

"Dull, isn't it?"

"I've had enough of the other kind to last me out my life long, sir."

"I'd like a fresh cup of coffee, Beaman."

"Thank you, sir."

The fellow went out and was a long time at it, and when the door opened it was Nora who came in, the silver coffee pot in her hand.

"A man telephoned, Mr. Potter. He says you have the theater."

Marie's voice was carefully noncommittal. The aloofness of her pale gaze conveyed nothing except suppression. "He said to tell you that the other play is closing tomorrow. He's holding the theater. But if you want he can let somebody go in for a couple weeks until you need it."

Henry Potter lifted his head from the papers he was studying. An auxiliary company in Brussels wanted to expand. A few weeks ago he would have refused. Belgium was a small country, its problems heroic to its size. The explosion of the Belgian Congo was still reverberating. It was no time to undertake new risks. Now, however, what risks could compare to his own? Risks with money were nothing.

"All right, Marie," he said shortly. "I'll call back."

He waited for her to close the door with sharp emphasis, as she did, and then he took the receiver and dialed. The telephone rang endlessly and was answered at last by the lazy voice of the blonde.

"Offices Sidney Vallant speaking."

He could hear the click of the gum in her mouth. "What's this about a theater?"

"Oh, is 'at you, Mr. Potter? Yeah, you got the theater. The other show's a flop awright."

Click—click—What was that tribe in Africa whose language employed clicks between vowels and consonants?

"Thank you. I'll take it."

" 'At's fine, Mr. Potter."

He meditated on the unbusinesslike methods of theater, one of the oldest enterprises in human history, the enchantment of seeing life portrayed upon a stage. It could not continue, he thought grimly, were it not for fools like himself, to pour money into it. He remembered that it was not, after all, entirely his money. He had demanded it from his subordinates. Never mind about his nephew Bob or his overpaid vice-presidents and managers. He'd been wrong to force his lesser employees to invest in a business which was made up of the tangle of human emotions. He had thought of it as a business, an investment, sound because he had undertaken it. He now perceived that there was no investment on earth as undependable, as risky, as foolish, as improbable, as this one which depended upon men like Aubrey Dane and women like Elena. And that Liz who sat in the office and guarded Dane like a jealous old bitch dog! He averted his eyes by habit when he passed her.

What the hell am I doing among these characters? he inquired of himself. Upon the inquiry he wheeled about in the big chair where he sat this morning in his own office and faced again the city. It had all begun that night of his birthday party. A few weeks ago—could it have been only a few weeks? Ten weeks, to be exact, and in four weeks the play was due to open on Broadway—this mushroom sort of enterprise, springing out of nothing more tangible than a middle-aged discontent on his part and a young man's ambition, had taken complete possession of his time and his thought. He looked across the city, today a pale and misty ghost city under a rainy sky, and he felt no pulse of life in it except yonder, blocks away, where in a dingy theater a few people of no great value, surely, among these millions, played with the deepest most secret instincts of the human race in this most modern age. What was he doing here alone in this castle of steel and glass? Intolerable loneliness!

The rain was pouring down when he arrived at the theater. It spattered upon the sidewalks with such force that the spray misted about his feet. Beaman carried the umbrella over him until he reached the entrance, but his ankles were wet.

"Shan't I wait for you, sir?"

He stamped the water from his shoes. "No, they'll order sandwiches in on a day like this."

"Miss O'Brien said you weren't supposed to eat those sandwiches, sir."

"What business is it of hers?"

"Mrs. Potter said so, sir, before she left."

He stared at Beaman. "What do you mean?"

"Nothing, sir, except you wasn't to eat sandwiches. It's the bread, sir—lies in the stomach, sour-like, Miss O'Brien said."

"Go home," Henry Potter said. "I'll telephone when I want to be fetched."

"Yes, sir."

The lobby was more damp and dark than usual on this damp dark day. It smelled of mold and ancient uncleanness. He groped his way to the stairs and stepped carefully down each one, gripping the handrail. The light, dim at best, was entirely gone today. The bulb had burned out, he supposed, and no one had cared enough to replace it. Suddenly his foot touched something soft. He stooped and felt a girl's hair.

"Elena," he said under his breath.

"Don't speak to me," she cried with angry passion.

His hand fumbled across her cheek and rested on her shoulder. "But what's wrong?"

"I've been waiting hours for you. I asked you before to change the director. I can't work with Aubrey Dane. I'm quitting the show."

He felt for the stair and sat down beside her. "Now, Elena, you can't do that. The show's costing more than we thought it would. I haven't wanted to tell anybody, but I've had to put in an extra twenty thousand."

"I don't care."

"But you must care, Elena."

"Money doesn't mean anything to me. I was offered seventy-five thousand if I'd do a commercial for soap."

"Now, Elena—"

"Don't speak to me. I want him out, you hear, Henry? Out—out—out—and I don't care to see him even in the building!"

"Elena—"

"I've got to go to the bathroom."

She pushed him aside and he heard the patter of her feet up the stairs. He rose then and descended into the gloom. In the theater the usual darkness was lit by the glittering lights of the stage, the empty stage, and upon it Aubrey Dane was rehearsing without Elena. In her place was the poker-playing blonde, sauntering through her lines, as cool and collected a female as ever exposed her bosom to the public gaze. Aubrey Dane was working with fury. In less than ten minutes, nevertheless, it was clear to Henry Potter that the star was gone. Competent work was going on, Aubrey was directing from his brain, the actors moving at his command, but the play was dead. He searched the twilight for Stella and saw her in a far corner alone, her head sunk between her hands. She was asleep? He bent to peer under her hands. No, she was crying! She lifted her head and the distant light of the stage shone faintly upon her wet cheeks.

"Stella, what—"

She cut him off abruptly. "Where is Elena?"

"In her usual retreat—the bathroom."

"Let me pass, please."

He drew back in his seat and she passed him and went out. In a few minutes she was back again with Elena. Like a child, she led Elena by the hand to the stage.

"Aubrey," she called, her voice clear and high. "Here is Elena."

Aubrey turned and leaned over the edge of the stage. "We've missed you, honey. Where have you been?"

Elena did not speak. She put up her two hands and Aubrey took them and lifted her to the stage.

"Don't make me do the love scene again, Tootles," she said piteously.

"No, darling."

"I can't do it again."

"No need, sweetheart. You do it beautifully."

"Do I really, Tootles?"

"Really."

"You're sweet."

"We can't do without you, darling."

"You're not just saying something to make me feel happy?"

"I swear I'm not. . . . Now do you think you can do the last scene? Here, let me—"

He took his handkerchief from his pocket and gently wiped her cheeks. The cast stood patiently watching, cynical.

"All right, children. She's with us again."

They fell into place obediently, docile, eternally cynical, and Elena played to the end, the same end, the question asked and no answer given.

"You haven't found the end, Stella?"

"I've only found that this is the end. There is no other—unless you want me to carry it to the ultimate. We could blow up the stage, leave the desert as it was before human beings ever crawled out of the sand."

"You're very bitter," he said, "and the audience wouldn't like it. People aren't going to pay to see everything blown up in an explosion. They'd be too depressed."

"They'd better be," she said.

He was silenced then and sat in gloomy foreboding. If it were any reasonable business, anything like Potter Products, he could give an order. But with these people! He continued to stare at the stage.

Aubrey stood to one side, saying nothing, refraining now from direction. The cast watched motionless from the wings. When Elena stood alone at last, silent, her face upturned to the oblivious sky, waiting for the curtain that was to fall, Aubrey Dane walked toward her, clapping his hands softly.

"You are a great actress, Elena." He put his hands on her shoulders.

"Tootles, please—" She leaned her head against his breast.

He lifted her head. "Thank you, thank you, thank you." And he kissed her on the lips.

6

Sometime in the night the telephone rang. He heard it afar off and he thought dimly of Ethel. She was calling him from somewhere. She kept calling and without opening his eyes he reached for the receiver, fumbled it, found it, and held it to his ear.

"Hello—hello—hello—Ethel?"

A gay young voice laughed across the wires. "It's not Ethel, Henry! You're dreaming. It's me."

Elena!! What other woman would so confidently believe that a man would know it to be herself and without question.

"What're you calling me now for?" he demanded. "It's the middle of the night."

"That's why I'm calling you, Henry! Guess something!"

"I'm asleep, I tell you."

"Guess who I'm in bed with—"

He woke suddenly and altogether. He sat up. "Elena, be ashamed of yourself!"

"He's asleep—God, I've seen men sleep, but this one—"

"Elena, be quiet."

"I have to tell someone, Henry."

"I won't listen—"

"You're jealous—because he's Tootles."

"Elena, you're a bitch."

She laughed again. "I'm so happy, Henry. I have

to tell you. Everything will be all right now. You'll see. The play will be a hit."

He hung up from her laughter. In the darkness he fought against a self he did not know. Yes, he knew, but he thought it vanquished. Here it was again, a monster, an animal jealousy, fury of the flesh, inhuman forces in his blood, atavism hateful to his reason. His glands swelled against his will, and he could not sleep for seeing Elena, as she must look at this moment.

Oh damn, he growled at last. He got up and fumbled for his slippers and could not find them and padded barefoot to the bathroom to step in the tub. He hated cold water in the tub or in the sea, but he turned the cold water faucet on full and stood gasping and frozen until he shivered and shrank. Then he crawled out of the tub and wiped himself dry and wrapped himself in his gray flannel bathrobe.

Only now did he allow himself to reach for the telephone. He dialed and when the distant receiver was lifted he spoke gently.

"Stella?"

"Yes?"

The quick, crisp voice betrayed no knowledge of evil.

"May I have breakfast with you?"

"Who—oh, Henry Potter? Is something wrong?"

"I don't know. I'd like to find out—from you."

"Should I worry?"

"Not until we meet. Then you can decide."

"You frighten me. I shan't be able to sleep. What time is it?"

"Half past six."

"Is an hour from now—"

"Quite all right. The earlier the better. Shall I come to you?"

"Please."

She hung up and he dressed and paced the floor while the morning sun climbed up between the towers of the city. With a woman less honest, he would have kept prudently silent concerning Elena's call. But Stella was honest, she was brave, and to be silent to her now would have been to lie, and to lie he would not descend. Long ago he had discovered lying to be the refuge of the weak and therefore of the inferior.

He had never been at Aubrey Dane's home, and he felt a shy strangeness at entering the place where Stella lived. It was a narrow house squeezed between two large buildings, a small two-story dwelling, built it seemed by accident because there had been a space, a few feet left empty. He could see a minuscule entrance hall, two small rooms and a stair when Stella opened the door. She was neatly dressed in a green suit, her dark hair brushed and her face fresh and calm. Only her eyes were wary, the clear gray eyes, the most honest eyes, he thought, that he had ever looked into on a sunny morning. The little house was quiet and she was alone, he supposed. There was a smell of bacon broiling, and coffee ready to pour.

"Come in," she said. "It's good of you."

She took his coat and hat. "Did you come in a taxi or in your car?"

"Beaman is still sound asleep, doubtless."

He followed her into a small cheerful dining room. On the triangular table breakfast was set for two. She did not therefore expect Aubrey. As though she read his thought she spoke carelessly—or was it too carefully?

"Aubrey spent the night at the office last night. Liz telephoned me. They rehearsed until eleven and then he went over to Elena's room with her. He likes to work late at night and Elena's good about that sort of thing. She won't call it rehearsing. Sit down. How do you like your eggs?"

"Scrambled. Two. I smell bacon—fine. I haven't seen that Lizard woman for weeks. I don't know how Dane stands her. She smells."

She laughed. "He puts up with a lot from his slaves. He has her charmed, of course. She runs out and buys sandwiches for him, and coffee—does anything, night or day. Does it for love and never thinks of overtime or anything like that. Cheap service."

He glanced at her as she moved gracefully about the room, in and out to the kitchen somewhere. No sign of trouble on that face, enigmatic, and just now quite beautiful in the morning light. All very well for Liz, but why did such a woman as this, intelligent, an intellectual, actually, allow herself to be charmed, too, by an Aubrey Dane? Unexplainable, except in the terms upon which he had been compelled to deal with his own instincts so harshly in the dim gray of the dawn, a few hours ago!

"Orange juice?" she inquired.

"Please."

"Then I'll sit down, and you please will eat first or talk first, as you wish. I am quite prepared."

He smiled over the glass of orange juice, and then ate his eggs methodically, a slice of toast, hot and brown, and drank one cup of coffee. She drank coffee and ate a slice of toast, and then poured herself a glass of orange juice to sip.

"Now," she said. "I think I have reached the end of my endurance. Please tell me straight. What happened in the night?"

He put down his cup and wiped his lips with his napkin, noticing in the stupid way one does notice, he thought, a detail irrelevant in the midst of tragedy, that the napkin was the same heavy linen cloth which Ethel demanded for their own table. But this was a small square—oh God, what did it matter?

"This morning," he said, "the telephone woke me. It was Elena. She called me, for what reason I do not know, to tell me that she and Aubrey had spent the night together."

He spoke these words as tonelessly as he might have announced a change in the weather and allowed her a moment before he looked at her. When he did, he saw her face drained white, her gray eyes black beneath their dark straight brows.

"My dear," he said. "I am very sorry. Perhaps I should not have told you. My instinct is to help you, and only truth helps—at least with people like you and me."

She wet her lips but when she spoke he knew they were dry again and her tongue was dry and her words were blurred with the dryness of her mouth.

"I am glad you told me," she said. "I think I knew it anyway. But I want to know everything that he is. I know so much—that I might as well know everything."

"I have an idea that it doesn't mean as much to him as it would to me—in his place," he said.

Her hands, clasped on the table, were trembling. She saw him look and she took up her cup in both hands. Over its brim she spoke with the same trembling blur in her words.

"Whatever it means to him—I don't know. But it means to me—the same that it would mean to any real woman."

She drank a swallow of coffee. "I wish," she said indistinctly, "I wish that I had met and married someone like you—someone able to—to love. I feel—sorry for Aubrey. He'll never love anybody. That's what keeps me sorry for him. He'll never know the greatest joy in life—to be able to love. You see, if he had ever been able to love—anybody—he could never sleep with Elena—not just this Elena—but all the Elenas in the past—and the Elenas to come, but the best that he'll ever have is just this need to—to know that he can—can make a woman yield to him—adore him for a little while—such a pitifully little while—it never lasts."

Her voice broke. She busied herself with hot coffee, filling his cup again, and then her own.

"But why?" He asked to give her time, knowing her need to explain, to ask for his pity, too, for that was what she was getting around to, he could see, his pity for Aubrey Dane.

"He's such a liar, poor thing," she said suddenly. "He was never an orphan. He had a father and mother who worshipped him. But he knew he didn't deserve their worship. They weren't even poor. They gave him everything. He had a Mercedes Benz when he was eighteen. He can't forgive them for loving him and giving him everything. So he invents excuses for himself. He kills his parents, actually, so that he can believe that he's had to struggle for all he's attained."

He controlled his shock.

"Somehow I believed in him, though," he said. "I don't know why. I don't know myself anymore. I don't know why I'm here. I don't know how I got here, by what steps—or where I'm going from here."

"Do you think I don't ask myself the same questions, every day? I don't want to write plays."

"But you've written a damned good play."

She agreed to this with a sad smile. "I know—it may

even be a hit. And what shall we do then? We'll never be able to escape."

"Could we anyway?"

"I can't. You could."

"Why not you?"

"He needs me to come home to—and I need his need. There's nobody else."

"There could be—you're young—and quite handsome, you know."

She shook her head. She spoke clearly now, as though these were old thoughts to which she was accustomed.

"I'm a one-man dog. If I ever leave him—I'd be alone for the rest of my life, all doors closed. I've been all through that—with myself."

"He'll leave you, you know."

She shook her head again. "No, he'll always come back. I'm safe. Didn't I tell you he can't love anybody?"

"And you don't mind this—this—this—"

"Philandering? Oh, I mind. In fact"—she was nonchalant but her lips were trembling again—"it breaks my heart—if you'll excuse the cliché!"

"I can scarcely call it philandering."

"What's the difference between a kiss or an—an—orgasm—if you can't love?"

"Shall you then not speak to him?" he asked, after silence.

She replied slowly, her eyes on the cup she was turning and twisting in her hands.

"If I asked him, 'Did you kiss her?'—or sleep with her—or whatever—he would say yes. He wouldn't think it worthwhile to lie to me about that. And I would ask why and he would say 'for fun.' You see, I know all his answers. So there is no use in asking him questions."

She was, he saw, acting playfully, with heroic effort.

He looked away from her painful smile and buttered his toast.

"It's cold," she exclaimed. "I'll make you a hot slice."

He allowed her the relief. "Thank you," he said and when she returned with hot toast in a white napkin, he continued, still not looking at her. "Putting him aside, I can't understand Elena, either. All day long she's Jennet, a woman who claims that love for one man isn't everything—not in today's world. That's what you're trying to say, isn't it? In the play?"

She busied herself now with the flowers on the table. "Perhaps I'm wrong."

"You're right," he said firmly. "You're eternally right. It's time women thought of something else than a man. You, too, Stella!"

"What else have we to think of?"

She poured a little salt onto the table from the salt-cellar and raked it with her fork. "Did you ever see the sand gardens in Japan? No flowers, no shrubs— just sand raked in waves around a couple of rocks."

"I've seen everything except a woman like Elena."

"You must see," Stella said, raking careful curves in her salt garden, "just because Elena is Jennet all day, and because I didn't let her sleep with Mark— I can't let her in the play—she had to sleep with Aubrey, my husband. And she had to tell you, so that you would tell me."

He cut his toast into small squares. "Convolutions," he muttered.

"Emotions," she said. "That's only another word for energy, isn't it? We had another sort of Einstein, a new equation, emotion times temperament equals the square of action."

She was silent for a moment, making her garden.

Then she brushed the salt to the floor with a sweeping gesture of her hand.

"There is also the possibility, you know, that Elena was lying. There is always that possibility!"

"But why on earth—"

She laughed. "She doesn't know the difference between dreams and facts, that's why. And so we must forgive her because she does not know. . . . Of course there is the possibility, too, that she is not lying. And if she is telling the truth, we must certainly forgive her for not lying. Therefore, in either case, what can we do except to—act playfully?"

She was so cool now, so composed, a half smile playing about her lips, that he gave up. She was too much for him. She had reached a self-discipline which he could only imagine. He rose, wiped his mouth clean of egg and bacon and coffee, took her hand and touched it to his lips.

"My dear, you need no comfort that I know how to give. I give you my reverence. But don't ask me to respect Aubrey Dane."

She smiled up at him, not rising for his leave-taking. "Wait for opening night," she said. "You have no idea what a difference it will make."

If Aubrey Dane noticed his absence from the theater during the next week, there was no sign of it. He telephoned blithely after a few days.

"Henry, are you coming to New Haven for the out-of-town opening? It's not necessary but you're always welcome—a bulwark, and so on."

"I'll stay here and attend to business. Chess tells me we'll need another ten thousand dollars."

"A fortune," Dane said lightly, "and be ready to see it evaporate on opening night."

"Don't talk like that."

"It can happen. This isn't a sure-fire play. I'm beginning to think I should never have let Stella persuade me to—"

"Persuade you?"

"It's hard for a man to say no to his wife—"

Henry Potter snorted into the receiver. He repressed a low impulse to retort that for some men it was apparently hard to say no to any woman.

"Not to mention other women." Aubrey Dane was laughing. "Women are so damned tempting! Especially women in New York. So many available! It's a strain on a man. They—tempt me!"

"I believe that excuse was first used in the Garden of Eden," Henry Potter said coldly.

He hung up on this and went back to his desk. The reason he did not go to New Haven or Philadelphia or any other place was that he did not want to see Elena. He had to sort out his feelings first. He was ashamed that she could hurt him, but it was so. He remembered the weekend at the beach, which he had resolved to forget and not repeat. But what had he missed and what had he escaped? He kept seeing her as she must have looked when she called him in the night to tell him about Aubrey, and why had she called him except to wound him and mock him with laughter? He was honestly shocked that he could still be tempted, and, pride still strong, he did not dare to allow himself to see her. If they met, would she not continually taunt him with that perfect body of hers, triumphant in its satisfaction, proclaiming his loss by every movement that she made, those studied movements which she practiced, doubtless, before the mirror in her own room, or for that matter before the mirror of some nan's eyes, until every muscle in her body flowed to enchantment? And then, because he was still a shy and decent man, in spite of the frightening depths he now faced in himself, he allowed himself to think only of her mouth, those lips that he trembled to remember, the rose of her mouth that he could never forget. He mused upon the strangeness of man's being and the nature of physical love, marveling that such torture could exist, his very vitals engaged and entangled without hope of release, while his conscious being, his controlled mind, the image of the man he was because he wanted to be, was determined to be, stood like a marble statue, without life, and giving no aid whatever in this crisis. He clung to his will to save himself, as a man, lost in an ocean without horizon, will cling to a wooden spar.

In dismal dismay he stayed in the city, alone among millions of people for whom he cared nothing, a loneliness which woke him again in the night to such abject cowardice that he forbade himself to take the telephone, to summon Elena, even to inquire where she was, in what hotel, in what room, a teasing self-denial when so easily it could be accomplished, and in the night even self-denial seemed specious, life being what it was, and nobody caring very much what he made of it or of himself. Perhaps it was Aubrey Dane who was right, and Elena, and not he, or even Stella. Yet he was what he was, shaped by ancestors and environment and his own life and he could only go on being what he was, doggedly, for to change now, whatever the temptation, was to lose his respect for himself, and that he could not. He did not want to be Aubrey Dane and he must therefore do without that rose of a mouth and that lovely demanding body. He was what he was—what he was—what he was—and having arrived at this final conclusion, there remained only the question, what was he?

In this maze, he remembered suddenly that Ethel had written him in a letter soon after her departure: "In case you should ever want to get in touch with me, Henry, Marie can always tell you where I am."

Without the slightest compunction at this hour, which was now three in the morning, he dialed Marie and heard her voice, after long ringing, very cross and unintelligible.

"For heaven's sake, who's calling?"

He inquired directly, "Marie, where is my wife?"

"Oh, Mr. Potter—why, she's at the San Fernando, in Rio, room 1723. Is anything wrong?"

"Thanks." He hung up.

At four o'clock, and why telephone operators had to act like dictators he did not know, it being their business to be on call at any hour of the day or night, he succeeded in getting through to Ethel.

"Where have you been?" he demanded. "I've been trying to get you for hours."

"Are you sick, Henry?"

Her voice sounded extraordinarily near, and he listened to it with hungry comfort.

"I want you to come home."

"Aren't you going to tell me what's wrong?"

"I just want you to come home."

"All right," she said. "I'll come."

He was about to hang up and found he could not. "Ethel!"

"Yes, Henry?"

"Have you missed me?"

"Of course I have."

"Why didn't you come home then?"

"I've been waiting for you to say you wanted me to come home."

"You mean you've been sitting there waiting in that hotel?"

"I've done a few things—sight-seeing and all that."

He digested this and then gave a gusty sigh. "Come home right away."

"Yes, Henry."

He hung up and lay smiling in the darkness and fell asleep.

He knew the moment he opened the door that she had come home. There was something about the house, an atmosphere, a fragrance. Beaman was in the hall.

"Madame has arrived, sir. Just in time for the opening, if you'll allow me the liberty."

"Good."

He felt suddenly young and hopeful, although an hour ago he had been convinced that the play, due to open on Broadway exactly two hours and a quarter from now, was doomed to failure. He had, in excess of anxiety, refused to allow himself any communication with the theater or with Dane or Stella and, least of all, with Elena, and he had not gone to the dress rehearsal yesterday. He had stayed by his desk all day and made Marie miserable, as he knew, with his carping. He had not even been sure when Ethel was coming—there had been some trouble with an impending hurricane, an outrage on the part of the United States Weather Bureau, he considered, so out of season. He had not made up his mind whether he would even go to the opening tonight if Ethel did not come. He did not like the way his heart beat when he thought of it.

Now she was here. He leaped up the stairs and then remembered what his doctor had told him. He walked slowly to her room, the door was closed, and he stood there, breathing deeply. Then he opened the door and went in. She sat before her dressing table in her white peignoir, as though she had never been away, brushing her hair, and she smiled at him in the mirror. He went to her and put his hands on her shoulders.

"Henry, you've lost weight."

"Of course I have—you've been away too long."

He drew her to her feet then and held her close. Ah, but this was good! This was what he wanted, this steady deep uprush of comfort and joy. He kissed her gently and then again, not gently. She drew back and looked at him, laughing softly.

"You're brown," he said.

"I've been lying in the sun, dear stupid!"

"I rather like it."

"What a relief!"

"Have you changed your hair?"

"Of course not—it's just that you never notice."

"Don't go away again—ever."

"Then don't let me."

She drew his head down and kissed him. "There," she said. "That will have to do for the present. What's this about a theater opening tonight?"

"How did you know?"

"Beaman said you had tickets."

"I have. I don't know if you'll like the show."

"Why—have you seen it?"

He parried, not too skillfully. "I've heard a lot about it. I don't think the critics will like it."

She looked at him shrewdly. "Let's see if we like it first."

That was the way it began, and the evening went on, still exactly as though she had never been away, to his great content, and he grumbled happily that he had not been fed properly while she was gone, the servants taking liberties, he dared say, and he too busy at the office—well, at a number of places, and anyway, the house was her business, not his.

When the curtain went up, he felt for her hand and she pressed his. This was subterfuge and he knew it.

Elena came on wearing her fresh blue frock, stunning in simple beauty. The crowd clapped. For a second he was blinded and his breath caught behind his breastbone. The scene was handsome and superbly lighted, but all was no more than the setting for Elena, her face glowing, beautiful as he had never seen her, and he was compelled to respond to the magic or the magnetism of the perfect form, the gift which she possessed in innocence, however she might use it and to whatever ends. Through the body she communicated and was not to be blamed, was she, if others longed to touch her and enfold her.

"Oh, how I hate them," she had cried on that evening at the beach. "They are wild beasts waiting to eat me."

"Nonsense," he had said, "people love you."

"It's not love," she had said. "It's hunger. They want to eat me up. They want me inside themselves. I'm afraid when they hate me, because without them I'm lost and yet I'm afraid when they love me."

He reached for Ethel's hand in the darkness while he stared at Elena. She took it in both hers.

"Henry, your hand is cold!"

"I'm excited because you're home."

"Nonsense, I never knew you to be excited about anything."

"Well, I'm excited now, whatever the reason. If my hand is too cold to be pleasant, I'll keep it to myself."

"No, you won't."

She held it between both hers and chafed it gently

while the opening scene gave way to the next. He sat motionless, dreading her first comment. She would not like the play. When he saw it now, new after two weeks out of town, he perceived it a complexity of faults. The thing was doomed. How would he tell her it was his doing that this play had ever seen the lights of Broadway? Yet the house was full. Elena could fill any house. People were watching and listening.

And then imperceptibly, so skillfully accomplished that he could not have told when it began, Elena ceased to exist. She became Jennet and as Jennet she drew into reality those with whom she lived. She created them as she was created, the two men, the children, the house, life flowing between them at first so smoothly, so gaily, and then rising in anger and anguish and passion as she fought against her own awakening.

He felt Ethel's hold on his hand loosen and fall away. He turned to inquire and saw only her clear profile intent upon the stage, intent upon the woman on the stage. She was biting her lip and suddenly she put her hand before her eyes, as though to shield them from what she saw. He longed to inquire—what do you think, do you like it?

But he said nothing. Not even during the intermission did he say anything. The curtain fell, the lights came on, people moved from their seats.

"Shall we go into the lobby?" he asked as he always did at intermissions.

"I think I'll sit here quietly," she said. "You go, Henry."

He went alone, longing to hear what people were saying. He stood in the dim outskirts, not wanting to meet anyone he knew, lest the question burst from him. How do you like it—something different, isn't it? And forcing himself to silence lest he have not the courage to see the raised eyebrows, the pursed lips, the shrugging shoulders, he heard nothing at all, no comment, no interest. They inquired of one another's health, of when this one was going to Maine and that one was going abroad and whether Tom had got his divorce yet, and why the stock market was falling and how much even a little mink stole cost nowadays, and how hot the summer would be after so cold a winter, and then the bell rang for the curtain to go up and they strolled back into the theater. He sat beside Ethel again and was grateful for he knew he could never have sat here alone, sweating it out.

The play ended at last, if it could be called an end. Stella had done nothing to answer the question and Elena stood there alone beneath the unanswering desert sky. No, not Elena—Jennet. For she was transfigured. She had ceased to exist. He felt a strange pure joy, an excellent happiness. He liked the play! It said something he wanted said and could never have said for himself. The people in it were honest people. There was nothing sickly about it. This microcosm upon the stage, this little world contained the universe, time and space, the earth and the human beings who made their home upon it, the handful of people, man, woman and children and the archangel who declared his own right to be. Everything was here in essence. He remembered the saint in the ashram on the other side of the world, proclaiming the whole human race contained in three, the essence of essence, man, woman and the archangel above and beyond. They had made it come to pass here, before his eyes, these strange and motley people, these few, possessing no morals, meager intelligence, certainly no business sense. Without any of the requirements for success, they had created a universe, from no material except their own frail bodies, inspired by the rainbow of imagination. None could have done it alone, yet in the most unlikely cooperation, bound together by ephemeral love and hate, they created life and he had made it possible. They could never have done it without his money. Money, meaningless except for what it could buy, and such purchase long ago meaningless for him, his money had fed them and clothed them and given them freedom from anxiety. Let him never again consider himself useless.

He relaxed, tensions flowed out of him, he had no desire to speak, even to ask Ethel if she liked the play. He waited, secure and proud, and when the curtain fell, when she turned to him and he saw tears shining in her eyes, he was content. She laughed half-brokenly under her breath.

"Silly of me—I haven't cried at a play for years—not since I was a girl and cried at something I can't even remember now."

He smiled and put her silver mink stole about her shoulders and they walked out hand in hand again, the crowd pressing on every side and they too in silence. What were they thinking, if indeed they thought at all? He heard no laughter in the lobby, no chatter on the stairs. But on the doorstep to the street, while his eyes were searching for Beaman, he heard a woman ask a man the question:

"What did you think of the play?"

The answer came indifferently or perhaps only cautiously, "It's not like any play I've ever seen. I don't know what to think. We'll have to wait for the critics."

In the dark privacy of the car he turned to Ethel. "I want to tell you everything."

"Not tonight," she said.

"Why not tonight?"

She turned and hid her face suddenly on his shoulder, unprecedented admission.

"Ethel, what's wrong?" he demanded but gently.

"Nothing," she whispered. "Just that I love you—terribly."

"But Ethel—"

"No, please—don't speak, Henry. I was so afraid that at the end it would go wrong, and it didn't. She asked her question and there was no answer and so she just had to make do with what she had, and when she knew that it was all she would ever have, it was enough. Except, of course, the hope that someday—someday, like the pot of gold at the end of the rainbow—she'll understand why she has to go on creating life—she alone."

"Is that what you got out of it?" he asked, amazed.

"Didn't you?"

"I don't know. No, I don't think so. I don't know what I got out of it except that I was so goddamned proud that I—"

She put her hand on his lips.

"I know, I know," she whispered. "No need to say more."

"Oh, damn it, Ethel," Henry chided. "You always have thought you knew everything about everything, and you haven't changed. Well, there are things you don't know and things I must tell you. For example, Elena . . ."

Ethel interrupted him. "Sh! You don't need to tell me about Elena either. I saw the scratches and I saw the way you looked at her tonight. It's all over with her, Henry, I know that, and we are still together, perhaps as we have never been together before. There is no necessity for explanation."

Henry was stunned. He opened his mouth to speak, but nothing came out. Again Ethel put her hand over his lips to silence him. Now, oh, Lord, she was laughing at him. Laughing and, and—crying—by God she was crying, crying *and* laughing.

"Oh, Henry, I wish we'd had a child!"

He fell back from her as if staggered by a blow. Now why this after all these years, when he had thought it long ago forgotten?

He said the only thing he could think of to say. "Ethel, my love, I haven't really missed anything—I'm so goddamned happy to have you home again—"

They embraced in the darkness behind the square solidity of Beaman.

They rode home in silence and moments later, as Ethel sat brushing her hair in front of her dressing table, Henry approached her and softly repeated over and over, "I'm so goddamned happy to have you home again—"

He kissed her hair, her shoulders, the back of her neck. Their eyes met in the mirror. She smiled slowly and his arms encircled her waist, turning her around toward him. He took the brush from her hand, laid it down carefully, and lifted Ethel gently so she stood directly in front of him. He stepped back, looking at her, acutely aware of the lovely curves of her body beneath the shimmery pale blue negligee she wore. She stood quietly, looking at him fully while his eyes wandered longingly over her.

He could stand it no longer. He fell to his knees, clasped his arms about her and sobbed, "Ethel, oh Ethel, my love, what would I ever do without you? You, who know me better than I know myself!" He felt dizzy, delirious, his head filled with the delicate fragrance of

Ethel's perfume, Ethel's powder, Ethel's flowers, Ethel's whole beautiful being.

This time it was she who lifted Henry gently so that he stood directly in front of her. Her eyes were still on him, and bottomless with love and desire. Unhurriedly she loosened the sash of the blue negligee and it fell soundlessly around her feet. She smiled and lifted both arms to him in invitation. "Take me, Henry, love me— don't talk more now, just love me—love me . . ."

In the night the telephone rang, lucky that it came when it did, he thought, after and not before the most satisfying lovemaking that he and Ethel had ever shared.

She answered as usual, but in his half sleep he heard her.

"Yes, he's here. Are you sure you have to speak to him tonight?"

"Who's that?" he murmured.

"Somebody who says he wants to speak to you on urgent business immediately."

"That's fifty dozen people anytime."

He took the receiver and she curled against his shoulder while he talked. He'd forgotten how she could fit like that into his arm, her hair in his neck.

"What?" he demanded. "A theater? Oh God, yes, I remember. I hadn't thought of it again after you said you couldn't get one in time for the show. But what are you calling me now for? . . . Well, it's late for me! I didn't go to Sardi's, see? That's why you couldn't find me there. That's for the actors—not me. . . . You mean you've seen the papers? What do I care whether the critics liked the show? You think they can keep me from buying a theater if I want one? Of course I want one. I like the show! That's enough for me. So did my wife. . . . See you in the morning."

He settled her head comfortably on his shoulder again.

"Right?" he inquired.

"Right," she said. "Whatever it is."